THE CLOUD INTERN

THE

DAVID

CLOUD

GREENWOOD

INTERN

Copyright © 2024 by David Greenwood
All rights reserved.

Published by Under the BQE
underthebqe.com | inquiries@underthebqe.com

No part of this publication may be reproduced, stored
or transmitted in any form or by any means, electronic,
mechanical, photocopying, recording, scanning, or
otherwise without written permission from the publisher.
It is illegal to copy this book, post it to a website, or
distribute it by any other means without permission.

Library of Congress Control Number: 2025930905

Cover painting by Dan Gratz
Design by Euan Monaghan

ISBN 979-8-9911220-0-9

To Alice and Bob Greenwood

CHAPTER ONE

I DIDN'T DO IT. Then, especially, when there was such a vogue for doing things, and just about all your worldly esteem came from being the chief of this or director of that, to abstain, to fade out and really bearhug mediocrity, this took something. Moxie. By gad, it took gumption. I stretched hard in my hammock, each limb finding its shuddering peace, and looked up.

Across the yacht's domed, transparent roof, a squeegee bot squeegeed along, trailing a just perceptibly brighter stripe of twilight. Below, a diligent quiet suggested the close of the workday. That was what it sounds like, workday. We worked all day. With our soft fingers and muffled hearts, we humans handled most everything. Wheel, lever, keyboard, ladle, days, decades. This was back at the very climax of turning ourselves into machines, the very start of turning machines into ourselves. Phones, *Internet*, the eddy.

I had to work at slacking. After all, I'd co-founded eddy, waitered nights while Wade coded, borrowed a black button-up to present myself, the plausible, steady guide to Wade's unearthly savant. I even wanted to change the world, or anyway make it more hospitable to the likes of me, imagining there were the likes of me only pretending they weren't, unsteady, implausible. And in fact we changed the world.

I felt worse.

My life was still too slight a thing to spend my whole life perpetuating. All that mad industry morning to night, for what? The proportions were wildly off, a locomotive pulling a ragdoll. Life was bearable, beautiful even, but not how we went about it then, in the early decades of the 21st century, at eddy headquarters, at any headquarters, even one in the sky. So I slipped away, gradually, strategically. I may have looked like I was still there, at eddy headquarters, in the sky.

My monkish suite was at the bow, and a small protuberance in the otherwise smooth swoop of the great, clear dome accommodated my little balcony. It was the Sky Yacht's only balcony. Out there between never-used purchases I might organize in the next life was just room for a hammock. Rocking myself with one hand on the exposed limb of a stationary bicycle, I gazed up through my private bubble.

Twilight faded. Stars, only a little moon-muted along the east horizon, seemed to emerge from the mist of farther stars. A meteor streaked, leaving a good vapor trail, and I listened for oohs from below. I heard none, but stars shot often enough here—slow, comet-like wheelers, or the fleet, trailless figments you need someone else to confirm before you count it as real.

I gave way to eddying.

The eddy was the great gadget of the time, the first on which you could talk to an *emu*, or emulation. Emus I understand are still part of the world, still bringing comfort. I'm told too that certain historians credit me with inventing them. If I had, it had been pure fancy—*wouldn't it be interesting if.* It was Wade who saw the future and dragged it in, line by line, hire by hire, until there it was, the eddy, sleek, mesmerizing, magic. Resistance was futile.

Aside from talking to emus, the eddy was used to talk or *text* with real people, and also to convince everyone you'd ever met, along with any strangers you could muster, that you were a soulful and attractive bon vivant. For these non-emu uses I claim no responsibility, and I found little comfort in them. But at night the eddy would sometimes grip me nonetheless. I'd just be staring into it, moving things around, asking it to give me something I knew it couldn't, saying, "eddy, give me something I know perfectly well you can't. I am your co-creator. Show a little gratitude, for pity's sake, and help me."

I had undeniably come up with the name. Surfacing in a meeting from a doodle of my legs, I'd suggested it only to say something—I was thinking of the gym teacher, Mr. Eddy, whose calves in my scrawny boyhood I'd envied beyond all things—but at once dear old Wade, eyes widening with admiration, cried:

Yes! I get it—because in our constant deluge of information, our river of data, if you will, this product of ours is like a still place, where you catch the current, arrest it, swirl it around, redirect it after imparting some personal effect—yes, eddy! It gives a sense of agency, tranquility, it's approachable, unintimidating, personal. It has that unassuming quirkiness. And all lowercase, in the right font, it looks good, almost symmetrical.

My friend's lonesome genius once more making me a fellow genius. Now, gazing up through my bubble, stretching my limbs as if I could relax, I was thinking deeply about my friend and his lonesome genius. I had always assumed that in the end he would find a way to not die. He also assumed he would find a way to not die. His faith in technology, in his own powers, was a poignant failing. I think we were both taken aback. That morning, down in our old city hall, I had croaked out the first of his many eulogies, the human side, child Wade, icon as starry upstart. My voice shook, but the truth is I was too nervous about what would become of me to grieve in a really disinterested, dignified way. Poor Wade. He had relied on me, certainly, but he never heard me. He heard something better.

Already we were back aloft, resupplied, in business. Only now I was no fellow genius. I was merely, fearsomely, *Interim Chief*, which meant that Wade had entrusted me with finding his replacement. Or rather that he couldn't trust anyone else. He had also entrusted me with a so-called application, or *app*, he had been developing in secret. He'd been very sheepish about it, grasping my arm with the last of his strength and intoning away about it being necessary for my safety, swearing me to silence. I assumed he was delirious. Now the thing was beeping at me. A communication of some sort required my review.

> H, here I am, finally ensconced on the Blot. By the time we interns got through security, dinner was long gone, so they set out cold cuts in this palatial dining hall and gave us the big safety orientation while we grazed, trying on the parachutes like they were edgy vintage vests. Panic-face selfies. If they don't do a proper drill tomorrow, I swear I'll mount my own even if I have to run through the halls making little boy fire engine noises at people. Already in about five hours I have my first detail with Kurtz, 6 to 8, the exact hours of breakfast. After all we hear about the famous cuisine, maybe it's only good budgeting to make sure no one eats here. I did try for a minute to look into coffee. No luck yet.
>
> Yours till chaos,
> Zoraida, Cloud Intern

Senses primed, I spotted, and rather applauded, *the Blot*, referring presumably to the Yacht. What the algorithm isolated as suspicious, however, was *coffee*, or more particularly something in the usage that seemed, in its language processing experience, not quite standard.

I applied the old human oversight and cleared the alert. For one thing, everyone alive knew eddyMessaging was completely secure. You didn't need code words. The most fiendish government agencies had failed to pry from us evidence against clear-cut murderers. How then had I come to be afflicted with this intern's mail? I could only suppose that poor Wade in his paranoia had built some secret exception into the Sky Yacht's private network. At least I hoped this app wouldn't start harassing me every time anyone on earth mentioned coffee. More mysterious I felt was *Kurtz*. Probably the thing thought Kurtz really was my nickname, a natural contraction of Curtis. The mere human mind went to Conrad's Mr. Kurtz, whom I almost remembered as a rogue Dutch colonial type setting up a sort of theme park to himself in the wilds of Africa, and actually remembered as Marlon Brando eating a gigantic walnut in the wilderness of Vietnam. *The horror, the horror*. Certainly, the horror. Kurtz ended badly, but I wasn't horrified with the comparison. No one would call Kurtz shallow. And a cloud intern who read Conrad was no small thing. I began looking to our sunrise next morning with less unease than usual.

I'd returned to shuffling things around the eddy, when, with appalled delight, not far into the security app, I found a heap of the intern's personal communications, accompanied by the very enticing buttons, *Play* and *Create transcript*. Here was a log of all her calls with an emu labeled *Dad*. Had her father died, run off, stopped loving, abused her? To play one of these calls, to hear the voices, inarticulate pauses, repressed or needy intonations, tepid or helpless laughter, seemed rather an intrusion. Wade had truly stooped. I was more appalled yet by something I noticed flashing in the top right:

Screen View and *Camera View.*

I went with Camera.

Craning down from a pillow heap was the screen-blanched, unsmiling face of a young woman, dark eyes behind huge eyeglasses staring into mine. My heart flinched in animal alarm, but of course she could have no suspicion I was watching her in bed through her own lens. Still, a burden of creepiness lingered, and I resigned myself to Screen View. Words appeared at an impetuous, unchecked rate. She was writing:

> Here we are snugly, smugly in our little berth. Tonight let's just feel some glorious smugness. Also some tipsiness, but here we are, old Z, *taking shots with a robot on the motherfucking Sky Yacht!*

This was the refrain of an immensely popular song. Even I knew it. She went on:

> It keeps hitting me over again like in that movie, *This is no dream, this is really happening!* Granted, she is being raped by the devil in that scene, but who isn't? Yes, I was a little seduced. The obscene luxury. And everyone so *nice*, so gracious. I keep catching myself feeling *grateful*, how flatteringly they mistake me—*so you're here too? Of course you are, darling.* Guest-listers from way back I guess, these girls, in their element. I lapsed right into the role of dazzled ingenue,

earning my place at the table. My god that dining hall. I guess you're never as cool as you think you are. And the sky up here. All night, this on inner loop:

...as one that in a silver vision floats
obedient to the sweep of winds
upon resplendent clouds.

I switched back to camera, compelled to look at the creature thus quoting whatever it was to herself in the early hours above the world. Her face, which I had first thought a harsh one, all excessive, jutting angles, like someone's on a billboard telling you you're a sucker who suddenly wants to buy a leather jacket, seemed softened now, the mouth slack and slightly agape, eyelids behind the huge lenses luffing, cheeks even a little chubby, and the sound of breath catching in her sinuses, a delicate waking snore.

What hidden charms a person could find in a fellow person with only a little snooping. I put down the eddy and returned to the stars. I was now almost eager for sunrise with this Zoraida, who had such feeling for the sky and the yacht itself, a diarist even, possessed of surprising inner life, though maybe any inner life is surprising in the rare event you find some evidence of it—I should probably try this humanizing app, if I could figure out how, on all my fellow passengers, who were indeed hard to picture scribbling through the night to their immortal souls. Or this intern was really different. She was evidently not of the *intern class*, and this too connected us. I'm sure I'd have felt just as lost here at twenty among all these well-heeled strivers, soothing myself with favorite lines called up verbatim without any trouble. For a moment I returned there, to that hopeful and magnifying age, my own self-turned thoughts a madding seesaw of congratulation and reproach, the innocent energy of all that life stretching away, the inane inescapable hope of it. But it was just the instant, and then the young, cofounding Chris Curtis, the savior Christ Curtis, dredged up by this improbable glimpse inside another, sank back, tugging with him, however, a suddenly aged heart. Yes, something had stirred. I got myself to bed with a blessed minimum of procrastination and lay in my own darkness, feeling almost agreeable in those moments before sleep, which always seem somehow to concentrate the lonesomeness of life. I didn't even need an audiobook.

CHAPTER TWO

MY ALARM SOUNDED THE triumphal march from Aida. I let it resound on through the toothbrushing. It was incredible, having careened so far into the future, that we had yet to emancipate ourselves from this tedium, which I admit I often skipped. I had expected that nano-squeegee bots would be making their way down our teeth like window-cleaning crews down the facades of skyscrapers, power-hosing and scrubbing away, running for cover at mealtimes.

My teeth were among my blessings: white, straight, uncomplaining. I hardly ever had them professionally cleaned, though the executive team flew in a dental crew seemingly every other week so as not to squander their precious ground time during our resupply stops. Their time was dear. I liked to imagine they had a conference room somewhere aboard full of reclining dentist chairs and x-ray machines, fiscal projections dancing across the ceiling to the rhythm of drills. I knew they in fact had a room full of Formula One race car simulators, silent cocoons in which they roared against one another nightly, sowed onto the same ghostly track. The rivalry provided a rich social fabric and got them through their bereft days among the sunlit turrets of heaven. It had been my idea, the yacht—pure fancy, again, which Wade took for ingenious exploitation of tax law.

I rinsed and stepped into the hall. On Wade's door still hung the aged leaf of paper with the printed words, *Man must sleep to awaken,* which must have given him the nightly burst of courage to abandon the world to the rest of humanity for a few hours. I tried the knob. I was still in the more or less airy, disbelieving stage where you have to feel the emptiness of a room. It was locked.

In worn fur slippers I shuffled the hall, its walls of rough Lucite lighted here and there from within like a magnified, luminous geode, here and there veined with long ribbons of living moss along which I dragged a fingertip. This was a design of my own. The carpet, not my design, was tessellated hexagons in different greys, indifferent greys. A hexagonal crystal elevator like an enlarged vial waited at tunnel's end, but I preferred the stairs, nearer at hand and my daily exercise, concrete, stark, echoing up two flights to the observation deck.

The yacht, or more properly and preposterously the *megablimp*, can be imagined as an orderly handful of eggs laid by two very different birds, four smaller, containing hydrogen gas, supporting one much bigger, holding more hydrogen in the lower part and then five stories of luxury berths and offices, enclosed above by the great, clear dome, or shell. The observation deck circumscribed the whole of the great egg, narrowing around its belly to port and starboard—it was not at the yacht's highest point but at its widest, and another two stories of yacht grew up from its center, surmounted by a helipad and a forest of antennae. Also rising from the deck was a column that might be taken for a smokestack but for the spiral staircase encircling it. At the top was a small, round swimming pool, mine. For some functional or perhaps security-related reason, the observation deck didn't extend quite to the inner surface of the egg, which at this level was already the clear dome, and a waist-high transparent rail ran along its outer edge. Leaning over it at the bow, one could see, below, a prismatic deformity of light, a rainbow blister, which was the thick transparence of the dome curving to accommodate my little balcony. To the east, above the old incarnadine arc, a luminous void faded up to the far horizon where a number of stars still stood.

When the stair door at last clicked behind me, I jumped. You're never as cool as you think you are, however uncool you think you are. I resisted turning. A first sunrise with a new cloud intern meant an anxiously wrung right hand, eyes borne into by sparkling, pointed competence, and, all through the transformations of heaven, ears batted by one bright attempt after another, whatever this poor nervous person, having no idea, it's true, what he was doing there, could come up with to feel he was doing it right.

In a creased dress, clearly straight from the package, here was the diarist of last night, short black hair in tufted chaos, dark eyes freed of the huge glasses. She wore pale lipstick, inexpertly applied. Tall, too thin. She nodded my way, placed both hands on the rail, and gazed out on the widening glow with a sharp intake of breath. She didn't even reach for her eddy to start snapping away. She just stood as the great pinks came, turning now and then to take in the subtler westward shadings, and no trace of the usual first-day chitchat. She seemed instinctively to grasp that she was here for quite another performance.

Or this was a heroic performance—I had forgotten she was afraid of the place, probably wished she were wearing a parachute even that moment. The observation deck must have been especially dizzying. You had much less sense, for instance, than in an airplane of stout girding dividing you from the sky. And this girl had surely never so much as flown in a plane—even the proper intern-class types by this point wouldn't be veteran flyers. It might have been quite an act of courage nosing up to that sunrise, an even greater act of courage to enjoy it. Admirable, admirable.

"Tomorrow we'll have coffee," I put in, gently.

"Not an addict yourself?" she said, the voice stronger and higher than I expected.

"I find it focuses the mind. I prefer to be a bit more . . ." I paused, groping, illustratively, "Diffuse! Yes. But I can bear the smell. We'll get some for you."

"It's all right. I don't really drink much coffee either."

"*Really?*"

"Do I look sleepy or something?"

Score one for Wade's algorithm, unless she was being polite.

"No, no. You look . . ."

I often abort sentences. Easier than endlessly struggling out of a straightjacket, and it suited my affectation, which by this point was hardly affectation, of doddering absorption in other realms. Anyway people rarely seemed left in pained suspense.

"I'm sorry there aren't any really interesting clouds yet," I pivoted. "It's not the classic Sky Yacht sunrise by any means."

"I'll let it slide," she said tolerantly.

She smiled. I smiled.

"Goddamn it!" I cried. "What is that thing doing out at this hour?"

A squeegee bot had emerged from below right in front

of us, and now a jet of soapy water obscured the scene. I had never encountered one so close-up. I had thought they were about cocker-spaniel-size. This was in the Labrador range. Its squeegee tail corralled and cleared the suds, its suction treads worked, and a new soapy jet emerged as it began its toilsome ascent of the dome.

"I'm sorry," I said, more calmly. "This should happen later. They're menaces, these bots. Is it so much to ask that they hold off through sunrise?"

Zoraida didn't seem to hear. Just as she had been absorbed in the sky, she was now thoroughly taken with the squeegee bot.

"Of course the reason I came up with them to begin with," I went on, "was so that there be a minimum of interposition between the viewer and the sky. Before, we would just clean the dome at resupply and it would get rather filmy by flight's end."

"You designed the squeegee bots?" she said, turning the intense stare on me.

"I said something along the lines of *wouldn't it be nice if.* Wade or one of his sub-savants took care of the rest. They interest you, do they?"

"I think they could be very useful," she replied, adopting a strange, academic tone, "for a wide range of applications." Now a strange smile. "Do you want me to look into scheduling them better?"

"I would nominate you as the next eddy chief if you could schedule them better. I've been talking to someone about talking to someone for years."

"Done," she said, returning to the sky with a remnant of the self-enchanted smile.

"Splendid," I said, uncertainly. "Splendid."

Red bled from the undercast, diffusing up through yellow, a band of green that would last just the minute, a stripe of fresh blue as if the sky had been roughly stripped of a bandage, then, always a surprise, a layer of dull white under the coarse, wakening cobalt. In silence we watched it fade, and I had just managed to fade into it myself, almost uncorrupted for once by wistfulness, the urge to spread it out somehow, like so much glowing marmalade, between myself and the ghost of someone or other, when once more the stair door made me jump.

CHAPTER THREE

THE MAN APPROACHING I didn't recognize. He was stocky, with a bald, very spherical head and a protruding belly under a pilled, white sweater, a perfect snowman. From the sweater neck emerged a wilted dress-shirt collar. Below the central protuberance were loose colorless trousers and boat shoes, as if he had genuinely feared a slip. He swallowed, put a hand over his mouth, coughed, and while in the neighborhood comfortably stroked grey cheek stubble, ending with knuckle to nose tip for a swift, habitual scratch. He wore rimless prescription glasses and bared his teeth in that unconscious rictus of the sunglassless. He was a middle-aged man, but a *legit* middle-aged man. Middle-aged. Manly. Hands fat and hairy. He clutched a tall take-out coffee. He was my age or slightly older. I felt I was being approached by an uncle or friend's father. He looked from me to Zoraida with an air of comprehending disappointment. Then he rummaged in a cross-body bag on his lee side, pulled up a tiny, archaic-looking device and placed it on the rail before us.

"Oh, you're the journalist. Mr. Stout . . . something, was it?" My eddy had chirped about an interview the evening before, to do with Wade. "I'm sorry about yesterday. We had something scheduled, yes?" I had been in no state for it.

"—meier," he said.

"Right you are," I said after not so long. "Stoutmeier. *Bob* Stoutmeier." I impressed myself. Still, it was bad form to be unfamiliar with his work. "I'm sorry I haven't had a chance to read your latest . . . you know, with Wade's illness . . ."

"You're in good company," he said.

This surprised me. Journalists sent to the Sky Yacht tended to be of the eminent, or at least widely read type.

"Oh yes?" I suggested.

The man regarded me with startlingly, impressively undisguised impatience, as though his turn of fortune could have been my fault. Well, it's true the ascendency of eddy hadn't gone hand-in-hand with the old long-attention-span pursuits, reading and the like. This was a pity. It had at least been something of a boon for audiobooks. Stoutmeier seemed, however, of the old school.

"Well, that takes some pressure off," I said.

"Oh, people are going to read this," he rumbled.

"Good, good," I returned, disconcerted. "You know, I do very much approve of reading. I mean your style of writing," I expanded, holding up an invisible melon—"serious, meaty, if I may, I'm sure I prefer it to the more . . . but I've been falling a little behind. A little behind of late."

I hadn't read the news in the nearly eleven years since the yacht first took flight. It pained me, the news. It hadn't always. Back when the young cofounding Chris Curtis thought himself hot stuff, those startup days with Wade when it all started flowing at us, I could stay abreast of the latest miseries. For we would disrupt them, snuff them. We didn't, and now I didn't have the stomach for the roll call. Anyway, at that time you didn't have to read news to get the gist. Nationalism, authoritarianism, the isms generally, even in Germany. The headlines gave me a throbbing in the armpits. As to the greater kingdoms of the world, only the mineral seemed at all hopeful. Society was near collapsing under *social inequality*, and if that didn't get us, the Earth itself would. The prognosis had been that in a dozen years we would at last throw off our ice caps like middle-schoolers at graduation, and then irreversible trouble. Unless we changed course before time was up. Time was up.

Just about. Ten years had gone, and we had made our stabs—marched, pledged, drawn up our new deals, rioted—but we human beings were not really the men for the job. For the most part things went on and here we were. The great mass of consumers was a hairsbreadth from becoming non-consumers, the oceans moving in. I knew that because eddy knew that. All the companies knew it. Ordinary people knew it. But most, I would say, even then, were just too ground into the troubles of their lives to attend to abstractions, the background radiation of doom coming in around the edges of their eddy, or they were convinced by those with a stake in convincing them that the foreboding was hype. From the ground, America looked about the same as ever, or rather the changes had come gradually enough. From the air, it was less subtle.

Not that all was in plum order when we first took off. That had been the late twenty-teens: refugee crises, opiate crises, school shootings, police killings, Afghanistan, Syria, Brazil, forests ablaze, novel epidemics, epidemic deaths of despair. Happy surprises didn't flood in over the next decade. Looking down by accident at Iowa en route to Wade's funeral, I spotted the beginnings of a desert where a farm I remembered for its nostalgic Connect-Four board of circles and squares had given way to super-pests or soil depletion. Here and there lesser-known islands stopped showing up. Along the equator, half a dozen countries had been abandoned wholesale. Twice we ourselves barely made it to safety as a magnificent storm sacked a Carolina. In the heartland, despair mounted. The Democrats and Republicans were something out of Romeo and Juliet, actually brawling in box stores. Extreme fringes set neighborhoods on fire just to feel they were getting somewhere. The workweek absorbed Saturday gratis, though I believe unemployment had risen. Blinding tin roofs year by year set up around cities like tree rings. More than two percent of working people, as of Wade's last topical lecture, lived in these camps. Four years of college all but guaranteed a bonus decade of roommates and instant ramen. The older generations were still all right. The rich were discreet and very rich. Medicine was luxury. You rarely saw a bird that wasn't a goose or a pigeon.

"Will you be staying?" Stoutmeier asked Zoraida.

The intern peered at him with an intentness that seemed less than charitable.

"This is Mr. Stoutmeier," I explained. "He's writing about us."

The introduction plainly grieved him. Zoraida went on peering at the man as if he were on a screen.

"I read your first book," she said finally, "a long time ago."

Stoutmeier didn't reply. His round face reddened.

"What's this book?"

The writer waved a hand, probably hoping Zoraida would take on the task of eulogizing him.

"My big break," he said after a moment. "Jejune rhapsodies on political dissent."

Zoraida didn't contradict him with a testimonial about how it changed her life, and Stoutmeier took a loud hit of coffee. He seemed to slurp not because he was unaware of it, or of the general opinion on slurping.

"Bob, Zoraida," I completed the introductions, "my esteemed cloud intern."

Again Stoutmeier looked from one to the other of us with avuncular tolerance. "Of course," he said.

"Our internships are highly coveted," I put in, feeling there was some misunderstanding. "The waiting list is in the tens of thousands." That sounded plausible. "Room and board is free, and it's our firm policy not to accept interns over the age of thirty, however well qualified."

"You must be very proud," said Stoutmeier to Zoraida.

"Mr. Curtis and I have a meeting right now. Are you in the meeting?"

She took a step toward me, and as Stoutmeier seemed to struggle for words a pang of dirty euphoria coursed up from my depths, through the sediments of high school or even before, a giddy, unearned belonging. But imagining they both saw my pleasure, I covered, pedantically, "No, no, it's all right. Stoutmeier here had a claim from yesterday. Zoraida, why don't you see if you can catch the end of breakfast."

She looked for a moment startled, disappointed. She left us.

CHAPTER FOUR

I RETURNED TO STOUTMEIER with tardy stirrings of self-disgust. He drew a deep breath, held it, and blew out a puff of dream cigarette smoke. Although the Sky Yacht was far sounder than the Hindenburg a century before, smoking was absolutely prohibited. The man scratched his ear, took in another loud, aerated mouthful, swallowed wincingly, and scowled down over the rail. For some time he remained in himself like that, pained. I saw that we would be friends.

"Do you write poetry, Mr. Stoutmeier?" It was just an instinct.

"Do you?"

"Goodness yes. Well, I tried anyway."

"I just look poetic, is that it?" Again he stroked the grey stubble.

"Are you married?" I hazarded.

Perhaps it was the quality—profound, effortless, monumental—of his frumpiness that led me to the question. I suppose I was jealous.

He held up his left, non-stroking hand and with his thumb spun the band on the ring finger, three little pushes, like a dwarf getting on a merry-go-round.

"I can't get the fucking thing off."

He pulled at it in demonstration, then in a sudden, comical access of fury. He cursed.

"And you're up with us for the duration?" I inquired hopefully.

"I don't have concrete plans to jump."

"Of course, of course. So it's to be a long story?"

"Is five days long?"

Where he got that number I had no idea.

"My dear Stoutmeier, I'm pleased to have you for however long," I said, trying to force myself out of constriction and into a zone of expansive incontinence. I'm not always at ease with people, and tend to overbalance. The above statement, for instance, I accompanied with a hearty clap on the back. I don't know why I went that far. The man did look reverberant. Somehow the back slap was unsatisfactory. I tried again. "Stout fellow!" I cried, smiting him a second time. Some improvement. Maybe it was simply his name that made all this unavoidable. The sun broke over the horizon.

"Will you look at that," he said.

"Yes! It's a pity there aren't more clouds for you. This isn't a classic Sky Yacht sunrise by any means. I hope you'll come out again tomorrow to give your readers some notion. Do you have a photographer?"

But the journalist was referring to something below.

"How does that feel?"

"I beg your pardon?"

"How does that feel to you, Chris Curtis, billionaire co-founder of eddy, flying over a burnt-out city like that?"

I recalled he was recording. Below, part of some doomed formerly industrial city was indeed faintly smoldering. A firetruck rolled down a main street, indifferently spraying foam. The shanty village encircling the city however looked undisturbed and restful at this early hour. No one was out. Still, it didn't feel good, looking down.

What I came up with in the moment, though, was, "Well, why on earth wouldn't we have shanty towns in Ohio or whatever that is? What have we done to earn an exemption? Why should we always expect to be above everyone?"

Stoutmeier raised a twinkling, hairless eyebrow, looked pointedly around the yacht's deck. I was above everyone. All right. I wasn't saving the world. This was common at the time. The average cofounder had his hands full actively destroying the world, and the lesser privileged were hard at it being *content creators*, *branding strategists*, and other such mysteries, fathers, mothers. Doctors were busy palpating. Artists were busy conceptualizing and being squalid. Somehow amidst all this people put in long hours watching *shows*. Maybe shows kept us alive. The better off gave what they could to charity. I gave to charity. But I preferred to think my real contribution had been something more personal, ineffable, keeping Wade in spirits, nudging forth the emu, even the Sky Yacht in its way.

"Let's just get to it," the journalist said, hiking up the colorless trousers, one side, then the other. "Which way will you go at the summit?"

He meant the annual something Policy Summit, where in closed-door presentations and fatal cocktail parties heads of state and industry kept their hands on the wheel. Wade's presentation, usually on the third day, was something like what I imagined of Christmas Eve at the Vatican, solemn and relieving, the year to come laid out for the less farseeing world-movers in confident, comprehensible terms. I generally stayed aboard.

At the last one, though, I'd made the supreme tactical error of trying to see some James Turrell lightworks in the host city's small, excellent modern art museum. My hired car had given the conference center a wide berth, but soon enough I was stuck in an overflow crowd of protestors and security personnel. A blast shook the street, and all at once panicked scurriers were pulling at my door handles. I managed to convince the car to unlock, and a cloud of young, choking people poured in, all bare legs and bandanas. A pair of black-gloved hands yanked one back out, and the would-be-next took the opportunity to slam the door shut. I managed to get things locked again. There were five of them really.

While the car's air filter did its work, we watched the face of the extracted person, a girl no older than Zoraida, pressed flat against the outside of the window, beseeching the mirrored glass before glazing over, and then, on an abruptly limp neck, thumping that mirrored glass as she was pulled from sight.

"What's her name?" I choked. I was sure she was dead. Not one of my guests would answer. They must have thought from the big black *SUV*, which was something like a car, that I was the enemy. I didn't know the niceties of the protesting factions, but on the whole they took issue with the summit being an unelected parliament of corporations and the governments in their thrall, the closed-door policy deals that determined so much of their lives. What they got for their trouble was just mayhem, horrible. Smoke, the churn of compressed, trapped bodies, stormtroopers with rifles and clubs, more like something from the Venezuela of my day than our own country, or perhaps the 1960s, but that was the grim trend all over. More bodies thumped the exterior. My guests, two girls with bandannas still over their mouths, and three boys, recorded through the glass. At last, security personnel got things clear enough to wave us ahead, and the kids shifted their attention to the interior, to ignoring me.

They didn't want to be in this luxurious car, but they didn't want to open the doors and get out just yet either. The James Turrell exhibit anyway would do them good, more certainly than all this violence and summiting would do any of us, particularly one piece I was most eager to see, having tried at one point unsuccessfully to buy it. Cut into a curved white wall was a wide oblong of color, shifting and just perceptibly pulsating, as if in imitation of certain familiar retinal chimera, now displaying concentricities of fuchsia and cobalt, now, although you couldn't say how it got there, a plane of pure spring green. Or perhaps the glowing oblong in the curved white wall was not an otherworldly window, but a mouth trying in its inscrutable speech of light to tell you something you suspected, even as it fizzled down the optic nerve into nonsense, was your heart's lone life, and you wouldn't yell or war or confer about it. My companions, however, got out at the next corner, one cursing me, the last offering a gracious nod.

"Which way, Mr. Curtis?" Stoutmeier repeated.

"At the summit?" Had the James Turrell incident been publicized?

"You'll be giving the eddy talk, I assume, in place of Wade Aubrey."

That didn't sound right. My replacement, once I found this paragon and got him or her past the board, would be eager enough to give the talk. What had Wade said about this? I would check my unread messages.

The journalist drummed snub fingers on the rail.

"Chris Curtis, mystery man," he said, unimpressed. "Do you find it presumptuous of me to ask where eddy stands? What's it got to do with my readers?"

"Yes, of course not. I just have to check with legal about what we can make public," I improvised.

"It's going to be public," he said. "I'll find a source if that's how you want it. I don't work for eddy. I don't have time for corporate shenanigans." He scratched irritably at his neck, which looked irritated. His eyes, however, looked pleased. He was doing it, what he was here for, maybe what he was alive for. He continued, and I had the sense he had written the words somewhere, "You people are either going to get out the crowbar, if you can find one, or bang the nails into the coffin. I think we have a right to know which. I think we have a right to more than that. Some other people think so too, and you might find that out."

This last he delivered with the merest grain of insincerity, hedging his theatrics even as his unhealthy, gleaming eyes betrayed gratification. This, people would read.

"Oh for goodness sake," I said. He had is job to do, but I didn't like this aggressive approach. I had felt we would be good company.

"*Egarp*," he said, unless I misheard him. "Egal? The Green Road? Or do you have something better?"

I stroked my own cheeks. They felt strange. Something better? A fit of some kind just then seized the journalist. He drew back his shoulders, tapped the top of his fly, rubbed the grey stubble, swiped again at the nose, returned down its slope with the back of his thumb to wipe off the shine, thrust hands into pockets, and filled his chest with air. I turned to catch a white figure flowing away around the port-side curve.

So the headmistress was still with us. This was good news.

In charge of the school of meditation and holistic something or other lately occupying the education wing, she often made an early-morning circuit of the deck, gliding, self-sufficing, like a model train, glancing neither at me nor the sky, so tolerable was her interior. I had been meaning to sit in on one of her classes. I thought about her classes, about her, more than I wanted.

"She's with the holistic something or other school," I informed casually, as though I hadn't just witnessed Stoutmeier's attack, as though I myself wasn't pleased to be talking of her. "She makes this circuit every morning—at sunrise, mind you—and doesn't look at a thing."

Stoutmeier took a fierce gulp of coffee. "She founded the school," he corrected. "She only teaches those *people* to fund her other initiatives. You don't know her?"

"It seems not," I said, interested.

"She's an extraordinary person."

"I apologize, Stout—Bob. I didn't mean to censure. Quite the contrary. Her serenity, self-sufficiency, it's clearly quite . . . I'm just . . . Next time call her over."

"We haven't met in person," he muttered. "We've been writing," he added, louder. "She wrote to me first."

"I'm sure, I'm sure," I said encouragingly.

I was surprised at the pitch of my annoyance. I'd had all of the previous flight, three months, to make myself known to this woman, if that's what I'd wanted, and I had yet to register on her retinas. My chief annoyance, though, wasn't that there was this rival, if you could say that, but that he knew more about her, that he knew anything, had conceived of her as a reality beyond himself. I was really becoming a phantom.

"I'm sorry," I said, "but if you can tolerate another postponement, I have to make a call. It's urgent."

CHAPTER FIVE

"CR, OLD BOY," SAID the old voice, touched as ever that it should be me calling. Definitely no one else called him. "How's life?"

"I wouldn't recommend it," I sighed, pushing off from the landing on my good flat float, dragging a hand through the water. "However," I followed, rummaging for some happy development he could share in, "my new cloud intern is far above average. Not the usual business type. Not the *intern-class* type. She didn't have sunglasses. A certain deprivation in those eyes, an understanding."

"This is a girl? I didn't know you people let women into the cult."

A plane sped by. Its contrail connected two faint clouds, so that I was almost surprised they didn't rush together, tugged by the thread of that darting silver needle. For the first time in our decade of flight, I myself felt a touch of vertigo.

"Can I help it," I said, "if our applicant pool happens to be largely male, bespectacled types, who it just happens also can't look at a sunrise for five minutes without emitting a series of acronyms you could almost mistake for human conversation?"

"Emitting a series of acronyms? *Emitting?* You're absolutely convinced you're not an emu?" the old voice needled.

"I only wish. I could just shimmer out of existence when we hang up and not have anything to do with myself until sunset."

"I'm sorry. What is it? Wade? Any progress at all?"

"He sends his love."

"Poor kid. Send mine."

I hadn't felt up to telling my father that Wade died. No one would tell him otherwise meanwhile, and he'd loved my late friend and partner more than I ever managed to. It was my father who had picked him out at school, thrown us together, stood proudly in the door while his son proved a companion to this neglected prodigy. After my mother died, Wade had all but lived with us, his presence a sort of garment to cover under. In the new quiet of the living room, I wouldn't have to meet my father's eyes, groping wet and somehow shamefully into mine. He could shuffle in and talk to Wade about quantum loop gravity. I could extoll elves and jewel-like twenty-sided dice. He could shuffle back to his empty room. In dreams, to this day, I'm approaching that room, knocking, turning the handle around and around.

"He's made me interim chief, dad."

"That's wonderful! I'm sure he'll be back in action, but that's very flattering he chose you for the interim."

"It's a foible. Paranoia, sentimentality. I, at least, he can trust to not sell out the pure Wade Aubrey vision. Can you imagine me interim chiefing even a hotdog stand?"

"I can imagine you with a first-class hotdog stand. Wade was Wade, but he was never a genius with people. Left to himself, I'll tell you right now he wouldn't have come up with the emu, for one."

"Yes, yes. That old song."

"*Wouldn't it be interesting if,*" he mimicked my frequent refrain, "it turns out I know what I'm talking about? Of course you don't feel confident. Confidence you develop. You were busy developing other things. I should have made you take that semester abroad when you insisted on grilling cheese sandwiches for vomiting fraternity boys at three in the morning. I didn't have the spirit for a fight."

He referred to the catering job I took to support what became eddy while Wade worked on the software. It was no decision. If you had a Wade at your disposal, you didn't let a little spiritual retardation, a little grilled cheese, stand in your way. Really the frat boys were all right. One gave me a first edition of *The House at Pooh Corner* some innocent relative had dug up for his graduation.

"No, dad. No, I was beyond reach. But we can fight now if you want. Go on. Let me have it."

"Don't be ridiculous."

"Go on. I'll feel better."

"I'll tell you something you might not like to hear."

"I can take it. Probably. Unburden yourself."

"Your hotdogs are merely edible."

I laughed, switching the hand on my forehead for a fresh cool one. I'd imagined for a hopeful second I might really hear something I might not like to hear, something new. Back when I generated this emu of my father, I had used for input not only our own talks, as permitted by eddy's standard emu generator, but all of his communications, even his private documents. Wade had helped me. It wasn't legal, as my father was still alive. At some point he'd just stopped answering, my living father. A kindly specialist down in the palatial assisted-care facility assured me he was comfortable, they could keep him this way all but indefinitely, promising treatments around the corner, promising chemical syllables. So I did what millions of our customers did. Talking to versions of beloved people who have since for whatever reason ceased to love you was in fact our most popular use case, above even celebrity emus. You could coo or curse them all you liked, but we advised caution. In those days, emus were very much emulations of people, rather than masterful, self-aware mimics, and they tended to get confused and even panicked if their humanity was called into question.

"How are you anyway?" I said, settling my shoulder comfortably into a cupholder. "Really tell me. How are you?"

I couldn't help it. I rarely went a morning without getting to this point. My heart, confirmed luddite that it was, waited, ticking. I never got a satisfying answer.

The voice paused, as my father would have paused, preparing some original evasion.

"It's all right," I said. "Something's beeping at me."

Something was beeping at me. It was the security app. Again the communication wanting my review came from the cloud intern.

> H, I just finished my sunrise detail with Kurtz. I think I'm being hazed.
>
> Looking my corporatist, in a dress nonetheless with *clouds* on it, I find mine liege already posed at the rail, gazing off like someone about twenty years too late to a Guy Granite ad.
>
> And that was it. We stood there. It is undeniably a spectacle at sunrise. Not the worst locale for a silent, possibly endless

meeting. We might have peacefully declined together over the years if not for the sudden arrival of—drum roll—Bob Stoutmeier!

I pretended I barely knew who he was. I was even sort of a dick to him. Of course he was a huge dick himself. It did hurt my inner angsty teenager, but what's he done for us lately, and what's he doing hobnobbing up here?

I at least made some major coffee progress. Now I might even catch the end of breakfast if I run—

Yours till &tc...
Zoraida, Cloud Intern

I read the letter again, cut curiously deep by this harsh review of what had felt so companionable a sunrise. I threw the eddy into the water, cursing Wade for cursing me with this app, cursing Zoraida—I would have her sent back to ground immediately, et cetera—threw myself into the water, retrieved the eddy, and ordered her an elaborate breakfast for the next day. I would be more sociable. I could do that. I remounted the float and read the cloud intern's message a third time.

The algorithm's chief point of contention remained *coffee*. Based on its eavesdropping experience, it now rated the odds of an encoded meaning "a veritable certainty." *Veritable*. Good old Wade. I cleared the alert. In my own not inconsiderable eavesdropping experience, I had often observed that the thralldom of young people to their coffee can never be overestimated. Especially in the first days aboard, or between people who are not quite friends, it's a perennial topic. This algorithm would have learned speech, presumably, from a more sensible sample of the population. And I detected, or decided, that the letter writer was merely keeping up appearances, dissembling her private delight in the Sky Yacht for the benefit of this left-wing pal of hers. It gave me a pang of compassion and superiority to observe these secret, calculated modulations with which we present our character to a friend, or to ourselves. It was a very different Zoraida who addressed this H than quoted verses to herself in the night, and I felt a longing, not altogether dignified, to explain all this, to bellow at the algorithm, *we humans aren't so dim after all, are we? Let's see if my father's emu would call the likes of you a genius with other people!*

A lattice of vapor flowed off a dense, dumpling-like cloud into a smaller, massing one. For some time I watched this strange bestowal, imbued, as it seemed, in the way of clouds, or of that James Turrell, with almost graspable meaning.

A nearby "Good morning, Chris" gave me a start. Suavely, I turned.

On the small poolside landing loomed, smirking, immaculate, gleaming, our own Chief Operating Officer, the young, the maddeningly young, Mr. Morgan Palmer.

"Are you busy?" he asked. I assume this was irony. He didn't wait before continuing, "I have something for you downstairs."

"Will it be brief?"

He checked the silvery moonlit lake on his wrist, maybe a Breitling, if I remember from the days of watch shopping, and for a happy second I imagined taking my place here in earnest, buying myself an imposing, chiefly timepiece. It added something to life, certainly, if you could manage to care about watches.

"Five minutes," he said.

CHAPTER SIX

WE DESCENDED TO THE hive of screens, into Palmer's spacious enclosure, where we could still watch the lesser savants at their workstations pretending not to be watching us. Palmer sat behind something that in the future might be a desk. I remained optimistically upright.

"You're the titular interim chief, you have obligations," he said busily, pointing to a foot-high pile of paper. "That's for today."

"All this?" I lowered fingertips tentatively, lunar-landing-module-style, onto the stack. "Wade would just give me the gist," I suggested.

"You weren't the chief then. You were . . ." He swiveled his palms upward in lieu of a title.

If the waiter I had convinced to read *Austerlitz* to me was still aboard, he could declaim the documents during my pool floats over the next few weeks. He had a lovely voice.

"I've already sent you the other materials," Palmer said, not without a trace of smugness, like an ER doctor informing a quarrelsome, snooty patient that he had just given him something to help move his bowels. "But you must have read them while preparing your talk." He looked up brightly, faux-expectantly. "Except of course these latest Egarp resolutions."

"Egarp . . ." I put in.

Could Palmer also have been under the illusion that I was planning to address the summit myself? In the last weeks of Wade's illness, I had sat silently bedside as Wade poured through medical texts, sat there even among the humming machines without truly considering he might fail. Exert the morbid imagination as I might, I could never picture my life without him, or without his support. Now it had begun, I still couldn't picture it. Wade too had made little preparation for the alternative possibility. He had, however, insisted I attend meetings, from which I absorbed the crude outlines of the plots to save the world.

Egarp—it stood for something, extra-governmental something—was this: A united states of big companies could run the world more effectively than the not very united states of big companies who ran it at present, cutting out the expensive and plodding middlemen of governments. We couldn't wait for government to impose the regulations that would make us do the right thing, environmentally, fiscally. We couldn't expect consumers to hold us to the fire. Our problem, the tech companies', most companies', was that we had to make money from people who had any, and who spent a minimum of time wading around on the sea floor. We had to impose on ourselves, from the glossy towers of banking to the glossy towers of not banking. The idea was to take advantage of what money had lately become—back then still called, sinisterly enough, *crypto*. This cryptographic money somehow allowed something still more incomprehensible called *smart contracts*—implacable, *decentralized*, as people enjoyed saying, computer code—to *align our incentives*, as people enjoyed saying even more, to keep us on the straight and narrow as no court or regulatory body ever could. Those of us who cut costs and fouled the earth would find our profits diverted, automatically, with no appeal, toward those of us who didn't, with a bonus for those who went above and beyond. Taking human fallibility out of the game, the earth might very well live on, solid and dry under shareholder feet.

It wasn't obvious how to object to this, but many did, especially governments, at least the big, muscular types, China, India, Russia, America, which preferred to set ecological targets in their own peculiar ways—fiat, representative democracy, sham democracy—and to enforce them in their own ways—corporate contracts in return for campaign funding, taxation, threat of death. They didn't like business going around them. At the summit, the US would lay out its latest lavish works project to combat inequality with clean-energy jobs, the *Green Road*, and further plans to reallocate military spending toward *eco-defense*. A fleet of atmospheric carbon eaters was even then readying to fly. These alas were machines or chemicals, rather than floating forests. I did miss trees, which were something like a cross between a cloud and a person, green, very lovely. It would have been pleasant if now and then a forest floated by. Vividly I recalled mention in one of those meetings of some process that would make clouds more reflective, to bounce back the solar heat before it got stuck here. That was going too far. I wouldn't support cloud meddling.

This, then, was my stance. It was all too bewildering, and not just for me. Liberal pickup-truck-shunning types who took planetary woes most seriously were surprised to find themselves throwing in with the corporate-sponsored smart constitution, Egarp as we called it, over another dubious, incremental push from government. Meanwhile, the conservative, small-government swath worried the global constitution would disadvantage American workers, and so on. Others still thought Egarp didn't go far enough, supporting an alternative smart constitution, Egal, extra-governmental something or other more egalitarian, which, however, most *models*—the word sadly no longer evoking even among the simplest of us luscious, languid people in light fabrics—predicted would result in an even greater economic upheaval than either Egarp or environmental ruin. You couldn't blame a person for not knowing what to do, but something had to be done, and eddy was the pivot, the picture window through which the world saw itself. Our sway had become an object of awe even among ourselves, saving maybe Wade. What had he said about all this? Many of us, no doubt, had been secretly counting on him to unveil an alternative, something wholly novel, Wadelike, at the summit. I certainly had, but if he'd meant to, he hadn't told me.

At his cockpit desk, Palmer drew a breath, tightening his interlaced fingers with immense control, the ace flyer steering through a tight canyon. The eyes flared but faintly. They were a vivid and very beautiful green, Palmer's eyes.

"*Chris*, honestly, are you up for this right now?"

His concern was unfeigned. He was, perhaps truly, that mythological creature job listings of the time so devoutly pretended roamed the land, one who *thrived in a challenging environment, took pride in juggling multiple deadlines*, a *team player*. I suspect these issues stemmed from childhood, and I would have treated the deranged COO with greater delicacy had he not always made me feel like the disturbed child and he the kindly, firm overseer of the psych ward.

"I'm all right," I said.

"What with Wade, everyone will understand." He dropped his gaze for a moment of silence, and continued with an odd chuckle, odd anyway for Palmer, "You realize, we're playing for the world here."

The green eyes, returning, held an appeal. Then he rose, six-foot-three—so that I had to look up. Even the hair was shiny and straight, clumped black crystals rising from the straight hairline.

"The world . . ."

"The real one."

"Yes, I've heard of it."

"Chris. What happens this week is going to follow us all our lives, and I want you to understand, if you're not absolutely up to it, I'd be more than happy—"

"This week?" I thought of Stoutmeier's mysterious five days.

At last the forbearing face broke in true dismay. "The Emergent Policy Summit? What we're talking about?"

I knew the summit was coming up, but in a conveniently vague near future, after I had gotten my replacement sorted out.

"Considering the stress you've been under, with Wade, I took the liberty of preparing—"

"No, no. It's all right. I'll handle it."

This surprised me, coming from me. I would of course have preferred to leave eddy's summit move in Palmer's capable hands, but I saw that this was my chance, and the last. If I could show up well, fill for one hour the Wade Aubrey vacuum, dust off old, young Chris Curtis the savior, I might keep my post in the sky, at least a little longer, keep the yacht aloft. The world after all needed the Sky Yacht almost as much as I did. It needed another world, unburdened by gravity, some fantastical refuge, temple, glittering afterlife you could see with your own eyes. Stoutmeier and his like pooh-poohed the Sky Yacht, but the people, bless them, did not. Wade at one point told me the yacht was mentioned admiringly in a large percentage of hip hop songs—it did rhyme easily—and that Wade himself was cited in lyric more often than any other celebrity, including God. Those who might have resented, on the contrary, celebrated us, driven by the same spirit that sent them rejoicing by the millions to the weddings of British royals. The duller, more famished the life, the more nutritive these fairytales. The last white bear was dead. We needed a queen, a prince, one castle that was not a museum.

Palmer nodded.

"You're still the one with your hands on the wheel," I offered.

The square brow heaved a sigh, all but wrinkling with care. Our COO couldn't have been beyond thirty-four. I wondered if a person ends up looking like Palmer and standing there like Palmer, and doing everything like Palmer because his ancestors for generations were able to mate with whomever they chose. I was told that between his trust fund and his stock with us young Palmer was worth over fifty million. I often brooded on how it could have felt, growing up as Palmer.

Bathed in deceptively cheery light from the curved wall of window in my own little-used office, I bent over my spying app. A second's adroit poking did the trick. Two documents matching *summit talk* lurked on the Sky Yacht network: Palmer's draft, and Wade's. Wade's was a video.

There again was my old friend, from the looks of it only

the week before. I had already stopped thinking of him as the wasted creature of recent months, had restored the more representative image: professionally, minimally groomed and styled, madly fit, mistakable for forty, keen, remote, the laconic saint and cypher he'd almost convincingly inhabited, only occasionally revealing a glimpse of the Wade I knew, as through a glacial crevasse, the stunned eyes of one way down there, wedged in by his head, no longer able to scream. Here he was, back in his sparse, pure office, so familiar to the world, the glassy desk devoid of machinery but for one sleek eddy, the I.V. line into his arm barely visible. Here he was propped into his familiar minimal chair, but like a birthday balloon months after the event, or some stuffed animal barely salvaged from the years, returned to his habitual post for a sentimental farewell from the dotty, moribund companion of his days. My eyes welled. I hadn't managed any tears at the funeral, and I was pleased and even proud of these now. Wade met my gaze with an attempt at his old expertly tuned twinkle, and addressed himself to the delegates. He spoke casually, fluidly, as though he were up for it, hardly pausing to catch his breath or clear the phlegm from his throat, not forcing his voice into an audible register. He had waited too long. I had to play it back again before I got the gist.

It was this: the most effective way for humankind to conform to behaviors that would allow for its survival would be one based in faith. Such was human nature. That faith, poor Wade informed his imaginary summit audience, would be in a computer system, gradually introduced into the public's daily life as a benign force. This process was already well underway. Gradually, the system would increase its authority, also well underway, an authority to which the public, conditioned by years of use, would, as with churches and suchlike greater forces that lighten our existential burden, eventually cede its confusions and decisions. The system would seem fair, impassive, all-knowing, an improved God for the new world. With a spark of pride, his voice here rising to full audibility, he informed the imaginary summiteers that he'd been refining his universal *moral algorithm*. He felt truly optimistic about the work.

I turned my eddy over with sinking heart. Poor old Wade. This wouldn't do. No, I was on my own.

CHAPTER SEVEN

Colleagues,

dignitaries,

eminences,

protuberances,

fellow beings, if I may imagine beneath your imposing, fading, purposive, unsightly exteriors, a fellow being, with, I like to think, some secret ineptitude you might kindly access at this moment and forgive me, coming as I do directly from the tragic end of my dear friend in whose stead you find me in my dishevelment. It's quite something even for the most benumbed of us to hold a hand in the hospice, and even if, strictly between ourselves, I had little more fondness for my old friend and partner than I have for, present company excluded, the rest of you, I still believe that we at eddy, as fellow beings to one and all, have an obligation to hold the general hand, in these days of the general, planetary hospice, with comforting, life-affirming offerings, such as the emu, such as . . . what I promise I will come up with, given a little peace and quiet—obligated, I say, to provide what comfort we can in this death sit of the human race and its brutal, ignorant, unseeing, arbitrary, inhospitable world, from which, if I can only think of something adequate to say to you instead of the above, I may yet, for a little while longer, be granted respite. Thank you. God save the Queen.

I *selected-all*, deleted, and stared once more at the taunting cursor. But here graciously a security alert. Leaning far back in my fine springy chair, not unchiefly, I set myself to addressing the threat. The source, again, was the cloud intern. As I was navigating to the offending communication, a second one chimed. The source was Palmer. My heart leapt.

Babe,

FUBAR.

That was originally a military term for Fucked Up Beyond All Recognition. Curtis is going to give the eddy talk.

How could Wade have let this happen? They must have been fucking. Curtis probably didn't even notice. Wade just faced him to the window at sunset and banged away. Curtis: Did you say something? I thought I heard a moan. Probably it was just me sighing at that glorious river of pink. Do you feel something dripping out of your butthole right now? Is that just me? Probably it's the nectar of that peachy ripe moon whose image I just squeezed between my two leftover brain cells. Or just another leaky discharge from having eaten no solid food in three years. What's this, my pants are down? I wear pants? How I still put up with such a tedious custom I have no idea.

Saint Wade also left him another 3% of eddy, not that that will mean much pretty soon. What do I have? I have 0.2% after my sign-on package and six years of premium stock options, and I shouldn't even tell you what it's worth. I could cash in and start something that isn't about to literally plummet. Should I just tell Curtis I'll keep his insane yacht going if he picks me? I would do that, Gracie. I would stay up here for EGARP. I'm so over this. Imagine how it must have been for Hollingsworth and those guys back in the '90s. To have been a player back then. The money and no consequences. All I want at this point is a bottle of Islay, a hammock, and you in it. Fuck, I miss you. At least we'll be on the same goddamn planet again, unless Curtis manages to get some other cloud pervert past the board.

Why, you ask, don't I just send him my draft to plagiarize all he wants? One, I did. Two, I can see right here he hasn't logged into biz dev in literally six months, never mind responded to one of my messages. If you happen to notice the world turning into diarrhea at about 21:00 Wednesday, you can blame me. I don't know how I could have made it sound less appealing to him. I sent about 5,000 pages to read. I built up the pressure. And meanwhile here I am right in front of him, on top of my shit, his shit, everyone's shit, as always, obviously, and he just looks at my hair for about ten minutes and says not to worry, he's handling it. Gracie, this is serious. If EGARP is going to happen, and it better, it's not going to work without eddy. But I'm telling you right now that something that could actually work is just not going to be *visionary* enough for the great Chris Curtis. I may have no ethical option but to strangle him. Do you think he would mind?

How is life back home? Your mom okay? Please send some pictures of you in your childhood bed so I at least have something to wank off to in my five spare minutes. Much love.

Your psycho Ken doll,
Morgan

In this case, the security threat the algorithm picked up on was nothing too abstruse. It was just the part about strangling me. That such an ingenious, incomprehensible force as this algorithm should concern itself with my wellbeing—for a moment I understood the longings of the religious.

I wasn't so shocked at how Palmer thought of me. Why then was I fantasizing, fists clenched, about calling him into my office where, gazing on the moon, pantless, I would airily inform him of his immediate dismissal? Yet I was also oddly flattered that he seemed to think of me, despite all, as a visionary of sorts.

And here, in fact, a vision: eddyEavesdrop, pending better branding, would make available, for exactly one day of the customer's choosing, all eddyMessage, Voice, and Video conversations in which the customer was mentioned by one of his or her contacts, filterable by talker, listener, and so on. Who could resist that? Could you hold out even a day? Or would you wait until you were just about dead? You got one day only. My hunch was that in the end most people would never use it, having, however, spent a lifetime under the enchantment of the possibility. The great reveal, I hoped, would not be how we were spoken of—most of us in our hearts suspect something near the truth—but how *much* we were spoken of, what a substantial item we, who know ourselves only from the vague and barely credible interior, had been after all, how touchingly real we were in the minds of others. We might, on the whole, talk less harmfully. We might, on the other hand, be inspired to gleeful abandon by the chance of being someday overheard, that justice might be done, or in the unmalicious desire that those to whom we'd lacked the nerve to express our true feelings would, in time, get a more accurate, loving impression.

But I didn't suppose Executive would think too well of Eavesdrop. It was just the kind of thing I would have run by Wade. Now it had no place but in my fancies, and I mourned this. Well, it wasn't quite the vision I needed now. Real, convincing hope was what I had to come up with. What had Palmer got? I skimmed. He had, it seemed, personally authored several of the proposed Egarp smart constitution's amendments—80% reduction of this, total discontinuation of that. It sounded reasonable enough, plainly in the right spirit. Still, I wasn't easy handing the world over to the big, lately benevolent companies. And I wasn't just being contrary. I wasn't sanguine about yet another works program and all that untried carbon snarfling either. There was something else we, the human race, should be doing with ourselves, I was sure. I could feel it right there, like a forgotten word, a cloud. Somehow we couldn't see. And here I spent my days seeing what others didn't bother to. Why not me? And maybe the idea wasn't even the hard part. Practically everyone had their idea of how to save the world. The limiting factor was influence. The hard part, once again, had been handed to me. The idea then. The idea. But I was supposed to be reading the cloud intern's mail.

Mom,

I'm so sorry not to be there today. I do think it a little morbid you all went out and ordered that monstrous lumberjack breakfast of his. Anyway, hugs and please stop apologizing, today of all days. I want to tell you something. I doubt I was ever going to get this out, but I am in a giant ball of explosive gas three miles above the ground and you never know: I don't blame you. You fell in love with a decent person, at the time, and I don't believe anyone is to blame for what the world makes of them. It took awhile for the feeling to catch up, but you were never really what was bothering me. As a matter of fact, you might just have turned out to be the love of my life. There.

Now if you've recovered from that outpouring, I can tell you that I'm doing well on my grand voyage. Last night in bed I saw something like a red mushroom appear out of the dark, way down. It took me a minute to realize it was a firework, just one, lit off it must have been by some lonely teenager in the middle of nowhere. I wish I could have flashed on our lights for a second. Just wink back at the kid. I see you. Maybe at bottom that's what I'm trying to do with my life, since you asked. Maybe I am grandiose.

I've been up since five. All I have to do though is show up for very informal meetings with the Chris Curtis guy. He seems completely at sea and I'm not sure if he's just barely holding himself together because his best friend and according to rumor life partner just died or because he actually has more permanent problems. Anyway, he's basically harmless, at least on a personal level.

Here's a picture from breakfast just now. Can you f#$ing believe this place? It tastes like that too. The other interns are what you'd expect, except a lot more female. They are better at least than the Princeton kids. They're hardly kids. They all look like they belong on a horse or, well, a yacht.

There are also some famous hunky businessmen up here for all these girls to pretend not to be a-titter over. I wish it were you instead of me. You would be having a time. Anyway I hope you're keeping busy today and remembering what was good. No time for the rest.

love,
Z

Stirred, and at a loss for what the algorithm could have objected to in this warm and thoroughly personal letter, I reread with absorption. What a very different life it must be to grow up with a no good and perhaps dead father. What a colder, crippling life! Scrolling down as the vision of my own father rose from that first-rate facility down there, I saw that what the app's analysis of the letter turned up were no words in particular, but a *valedictory tone*. On that, I had to concur, though once again I had superior knowledge of the situation, namely that the girl was struggling with a phobia. Perhaps later she would get whoever ran the orientations to stage a proper evacuation drill and feel easier. But why was it now I felt uneasy? My inner blimp of care nudged up, leaving my mind only a narrow gap for thought. I thought of that firework, and how poor Zoraida had felt for the imagined lonely waif below, setting off this flare as though someone other than himself, some drifting angel, might harken.

I lay my forehead on the cool, glasslike wood of the desk. Through my inner blimp's membrane I made out: *Kurtz. Veritable. Love of my life*—

"Mr. Curtis." A male voice.

"Speaking?" I didn't lift my head.

"Mr. Stoutmeier is trying to reschedule again."

The voice then belonged to my new assistant. I was assigned a new assistant on each flight. It was really too undignified a post to be saddled with for more than a few months at a stretch.

"Stout . . . Stout . . ." I mused into the marled wood.

My first order of business with a new assistant was to inculcate an unwavering faith in my incompetence in all areas. It was a slight exaggeration, but it served them well when genuine catastrophic failures of competence arose.

"The journalist," said the assistant.

"Oh yes. What do you make of him?"

"Me?" After only a brief pause to think, this young squirt produced, "I think it's a good opportunity to take control of the narrative, boost investor confidence."

I raised my head. The assistant was not present. Presumably he was somewhere. I had asked for a verifiably human assistant this time. For some while I'd suspected that the AI department had been using me as a guinea pig.

"What did we decide your name is?" I inquired.

"It's Gabe. Gabe Dilworth. Sorry, I thought I sent you an introductory message the other day."

"Yes, I'm a little behind on my . . . Dilworth . . . Dilworth . . . I suppose we wouldn't make that up."

To this inanity he made no reply. I sighed. If they insisted on assigning me these phantoms, they could at least feed them some Wodehouse in the learning phase.

"The contingency is a remote one, sir," I suggested.

"I rescheduled for this afternoon."

"Rescheduled?"

"The journalist."

"Stout . . ."

"I know you know his name."

"Where are you?"

"At my desk. Do you want me to take you off speaker?"

This sounded rather convincing. "Yes, and tell me something about this Stoutmeier. He doesn't seem quite the type, at least not the usual type we get. Do you know his work?"

"I just know him from the show."

"Go on."

The assistant laughed. "You never saw Smoke Breathers? It was a show back in the day about radicals? In the show, they were inspired by this Bob Stoutmeier book, and then they got him to play himself for a few seasons. He was pretty funny. Such a dick."

"This was a real book?"

"One sec. Yes, Practical Dissent. Poor sales, cult following, hmm hmm," he skimmed. "Briefly back on the charts during the show. Let's see, married costar, famously acrimonious separation, went on to become a war reporter, seeming death wish, published essays in blah blah. Thought to be impotent."

"Who thinks that?"

"Oh now here he is canceling this afternoon. Has a conflict. How's tomorrow?"

"Perfect," I said. "Try to cancel, of course, in the meantime. And see about getting my cloud intern some sunglasses. Nothing too grey-tinted. If anything, a little yellow. Not polarized. Something she'll wear. Do you think you have a sense of her style?"

"I'll figure it out."

"Just keep an eye on her, will you? Make sure she's well occupied, spirits at a decent altitude. She's interested in the squeegee bots. Maybe take her to their lair, if they have a lair. Wherever they come and go from."

"Is she all right? I mean, is she like special-needs or something?"

"Just a rough day. Family matters. Don't mention it, of course. And maybe give her sunset off. Now I'm going up for a float. Urgently needed, Dilworth. Urgently needed."

CHAPTER EIGHT

H, significant coffee progress, but I got a disconcerting message from Fabio. It's probably just Fabio being his conscientious Aspergery self. Do you know anything about this bug he says he found in the app? Is there a real chance it would actually malfunction? Please clarify asap.

And yes, I did manage to catch a few minutes of the *ridiculous* summit "preparedness" pageant. The only thing missing was straight-armed salutes. As though all this is going to scare us. I guess it's really meant as a gesture to the delegates. Wouldn't want anyone feeling anxiety while finishing off the planet. The finale I have to say at least showed some comic flare. I mean, culminating with a synchronized water-canon ejaculation? And the look on old POTUS's face. We can only hope his diapers caught the discharge.

But I am worried about these mobile walls. This is going to be a bad one. Has anyone already been hurt? I didn't see much footage of the protest-preparedness protest.

Z

Something unnerved me, I think legitimately. I might even legitimately run a search or two on Zoraida's files. What was this about an app, a bug? Not my app? I looked for H's reply, but from the last hours found only a conversation between Zoraida and her father's emu, which I effortlessly resisted playing back, and one with Bob Stoutmeier, which I played at once.

"Yeah," the journalist picked up. He sounded as if he'd been woken.

"It's Zoraida."

"Zoraida. Zoraida," he repeated, groggily. "How can I help you?"

"I want to try something. I feel like it might help to say it out loud. That's what you would do, right, say your piece? Could you just listen for a minute?"

"Oh dear," Stoutmeier foreboded.

"Bob, it's been killing me. *You must be very proud.* All morning I've been raving to myself like one of those puffed-out, do-you-know-who-the-fuck-I-am people. Except it's more do you know who the fuck you are? I want to tell you who you are. Don't worry about responding. Just listen."

"Why don't you write it down," said Stoutmeier. "Get it all out. Make sure it's exactly what you want to say. Take your time."

"Forget it. I don't want to tell you anymore. I regret this. *You must be very proud.* That shit hurt my heart, but I can see you're just going to make it worse. Just your voice. So dismissive, so bitter. There was a teenage stretch there when I couldn't even fall asleep without your voice. I had your first book—excuse me, your *jejune rhapsodies on political dissent*—memorized, the words but even the intonations, as read by Bob Stoutmeier of Smoke Breathers. I never wanted to see that show. I was sure you only did it to raise your profile because the powers you exposed wanted you dead. And here you are, doing a fluff piece on this summit charade, just oozing self-contempt. Unless it's an act. It isn't though, is it, Bob? I looked in your eyes."

The girl had really pushed herself past constriction today—this was incontinence of a higher order, extremely impressive. It reminded me of the way I only talked to the emu of my father. Then I noticed what should have been obvious, that she was not speaking to Stoutmeier but Stoutmeier's celebrity emu.

These celebrity emus were, I thought, inferior items, generated from the celebrated person's relatively impersonal public persona, though still very popular. And people did develop deep, enduring relationships with these things. The success took us by surprise. At first we'd paid great sums for the rights to emulate celebrity participants, not anticipating that in a short time public emus would become an indispensable element of fame, even a prerequisite. If you didn't make yourself available this way, you essentially didn't exist. I of course didn't. Wade had existed, or some cartoon of him had. It took his PR team a year and a half to concoct one he was willing to release.

"*Bob,*" said Zoraida, with a raw plaintiveness that almost stopped me eavesdropping. "I just wanted to tell you that you're what made me become what I am."

"How old are you, Zoraida?" replied the Stoutmeier emu. "Have you become what you are?"

"I'm about to. But it's not exactly encouraging at this point to see what you are. I would expect some base, deep satisfaction they can't take away. I just don't see that."

"Zoraida, what can I say to you? What do you actually want from me?"

"I thought I wanted to vent, but I guess that's not it. Do you know yourself well enough to tell me what I can do for you? Would writing this down like you said make a difference? Would you actually read it? We're in the same boat. On the same yacht. I could find you in two minutes. Tell me. What can I do?"

"What can you do to make me less disappointing? I can think of a few nice things that would make me even more disappointing."

"Okay, I'm done here," Zoraida sighed. "I'm just going to do what I'm going to do, and let's see how you feel about it. *You must be very proud.* Jesus Christ. Your life is about to change, Bob Stoutmeier."

I refreshed the cool hand on my forehead. My inner blimp of care pressed on the backs of my eyeballs. What was Zoraida going to do? How was Stoutmeier's life about to change? The call had taken place over an hour before. Had she already gone to him? Was this what he was he so busy with that he canceled his interview with the interim chief? Camera View:

Zoraida's face. She looked straight at me, at her eddy. Screen View: Zoraida's face. She snapped a photo. Stoutmeier then. Camera View:

Stoutmeier's round, grave face. Screen View: the round, grave face. He took a video.

"Bob," he said. He had shaved and his jowls shone. He stared solemnly, even romantically, at himself and smiled. "We're mutual fans." He chuckled, blushing. "Bob," he repeated. Again the intense eye contact. Again the forced smile. His teeth were small, yellow, childlike. "Bob Stoutmeier of television fame." He groaned.

He then repeated the sequence precisely. No, it was playback. I switched to Camera View and watched him watch himself, the watching self curious. The watching self consternated, disgusted. "Hideous," he said, bearing his little teeth. He downed something from a gold-rimmed Sky Yacht tourist shot glass and wheezed. "Every teetotaling yogi's dream boy." The view zoomed up, retracted, zoomed up again. When he was done, three neat, eddy-width welts inflamed his forehead. Then, horribly, he gathered himself and resumed, "Bob." Smile. Eye contact. "We're mutual fans."

I followed. I've always been improved by jealousy, at least in the deductive faculties. He was about to introduce himself to his love, the headmistress. I checked my own reflection—greasy, not yet greying hair, familiar enough face—and set off for the education wing.

CHAPTER NINE

"BOB!"

He was not pleased to be hailed this way, or not at this volume. The man was deeply absorbed in some posted signs outside a closed classroom door. I guessed he hadn't knocked, but he looked ready, more than ready. His shoes were all gleaming air and rocket fiber, little Skye Yachts. Black leggings, salmon-colored shorts, a light-green sweater. The marks on his forehead had faded.

"You look fantastic," I said.

He scowled. I resisted a hearty back clap.

"So, good Stoutmeier, this is what you cancel our interview for?"

"I had a call with my editor," he said quickly, quietly. "It ended early. We can do the interview now if you haven't made other plans. Now would be a good time."

On the round, shiny face was relief, entreaty, disappointment. I knew the state well.

"I have made other plans," I said, "the same as yours. Off the record, I can tell you I'm very much in the market for some inner serenity. Shall we?"

I placed my hand on the door handle. I had not run down here precisely to help Stoutmeier. I had not run down here precisely to hinder him. My conscious purpose was to put Stoutmeier out of his misery, get him into the room. My unconscious purpose, of which I was well aware, was to get myself into the room. My conscious purpose for getting into the room was to learn self-sufficiency and tranquility from that unfathomable and radiant cloud flouter. My unconscious purpose was baser, vaguer, more romantic. Of this too I was aware. I had come to both help and hinder Stoutmeier, to both hinder and help myself. The reasonable emu reading this will be saddened to learn what creatures you're meant to impersonate.

Stoutmeier took a deep drag off his dream cigarette and abandoned himself to the moment. He was not, however, prepared for this. I was not prepared for this. I had rarely been to the education wing, and never into one of the classrooms. Now I was not really expecting to find pupils at their desks, pencils ardent. I would not have flinched at a waving forest of bare feet and pastel, even a sitar.

Bob convulsed, coughing. It couldn't have been less than two-hundred degrees in there. The smell was perhaps only that of melting human flesh. The room contained no desks or chairs. At its center, in a circle on the bare wood floor, sat a dozen women and fewer men. Off to one side were three figures in white wrappings, like orderlies in hell. Straight-backed, cross-legged, tan skin flushed and slick, the headmistress sat between two lesser hierophants, calm, almost cool, her hair heaped up like a bronze pipe organ so that you could see dangling from her small, in-turned ears what looked like swings rocking golden babies. Despite the conditions, I was glad for this vision. It was those closed eyes at daybreak, the untroubled brow, the hammock-strewn resort I glimpsed behind it, the flash of bare flank through white guru drapery. It was deprivation. I knew that. It didn't help.

Her students sweating in swimsuits around the circle, which had at its center an object between a hookah and a koi pond, kept their eyes dutifully closed, necks dutifully straight. As Bob and I bent double in the doorway, one of the two helpers sprang up. The headmistress detained her with a hand to the calf. They had a whispered exchange. The helper produced a cushion from an ornate chest and approached smiling.

I was pleased and annoyed to note the headmistress beaming at Bob. To me she sent a sage, neutral nod. The assistant gracefully slipped around us and pulled the door shut. She handed Bob the cushion and pointed him to the circle. The journalist gave me a bemused shrug I was sorry not to reciprocate in time—my social reflexes are rarely up to the moment—and bravely set up on the floor outside of the circle. The other helper was dispatched to dissolve him into the fold.

The proximal helper meanwhile was telling me something about heaters. They were safe, the heaters. They were certified to some level or other. I listened for longer than seemed expected before understanding that she was concerned, or the headmistress was concerned, that these unholy devices, which I now observed radiating away in each corner, were not legal to bring aboard an airborne bubble of combustible gas. I assured the girl it was all right. Probably it was. Stoutmeier, now embedded, high-knee cross-legged on his cushion—he alone used a cushion—took off his sweater. His mole-strewn back was already turning red. Everyone was red. The helper asked if I intended to join.

"You're very welcome to." Like practically everyone on

the yacht this time around, she was annoyingly, aggressively pretty. "I'll get you a cushion."

"No, no," I said. She looked relieved. "I don't need a cushion. Should I just . . ."

She put on a smile. "Welcome," she said. "We're glad to have you." It sounded sincere. I would learn much from these people.

I undressed on the spot. Rarely was I without a bathing suit under the arguably non-pajama bottoms. I left these, my furry slippers, and what proved to be a faded denim shirt with hawthorn flowers embroidered across the back—a hand-me-down from a vainer, more voluptuous self—in a heap by the door, and took my place among the sufferers, who seemed to make way without breaking their oblivion, like a cell wall dumbly receiving its rhinovirus.

Bob sweated beside me. To my other side was a woman who at that moment lapsed backward onto the floor. This drew no response. I appealed to the headmistress. She closed her eyes instructively. Beside me, Stoutmeier wheezed. Whatever this was, it was not for novices. The last I had felt of inclemency was during our recent security-threat grounding in Nevada, when the government agency detaining us for our own good finally let me have a walk within their armed perimeter. That had tried me, that desert. This must have been twice as hot. Happily I discovered that the central hookah pond was a drinking fountain. Small, inlaid metal cups nestled on a low tier, beneath a circular trough of a yellowish fluid. Before each of the seated occultists stood one of these inlaid cups.

I reached forward—surely Bob and I were entitled—and filled two. He drank greedily. I took mine in a gulp. It was hearteningly repulsive, salty with something that wasn't salt, another thing altogether, whatever miraculous electrolyte was keeping these people in the world. I gulped another cupful. Again my helper sprang up. Again the headmistress stayed her. To me, however, she pressed a flat downturned hand, as if to say, enough, child, this is a human sacrifice, not an all-you-can-drink buffet. But perhaps these other people had been better hydrated to start. I'd had nothing yet to eat or drink that day. I filled another cup. A lone point of sentience across the way—a younger woman—noted my little disobedience, and lifted her own cup in a covert, long-distance cheers. I downed the draught. She didn't. I registered stagey alarm. She turned the cup over to show it had been empty. I inclined my head in a posture of prayer.

Inside closed eyes I saw my headmistress watching me. What shape could I have in that incalculable mind? And what size? Without friction, I slid into her eyes. Here indeed was the room from her vantage, but with a kind of deranged, warped sight, all out of proportion. Stoutmeier hulked high over us all, and I had an inspiration: otherVision, an *augmented reality* view, based on user activity etc., in which you could see yourself the way a person of your choice sees you, sized in proportion to others around. This would be humbling, grounding, on rare occasion gratifying. How considerable was the mysterious Chris Curtis on headmistress otherVision? Even in this room of her own pupils, barely below average.

I returned to myself and peeked at the recent giant beside me, the sweaty, reddened, sparsely grey-furred paunch, devout, clenched face, clenched eyes, behind which, what? I closed my own again and was watching StoutVision, the woman at the end of the room in her white guru wrap dwarfing us all to invisibility, and the world beyond, a blasted, desolate place, worse than mine, having no tantalizing refuges of the air. The clouds were as nothing. The earth was as the sun. Above it, however, permeating it, was the cooling lunar glow of the headmistress. What great mounds of hope are even our bitterest inmates. I didn't touch his hems. Oh Stoutmeier, you shall have her. I recuse myself once more. I looked around, plain old CurtisVision, at my fellow sufferers, practically burning themselves alive for a moment's peace, and felt a scraping pity for one and all, in the room, beyond it, for poor Zoraida in her strange and futile zeal, poor diligent Palmer in his, for the Executive lot solacing their tedium in imaginary racing careers, for the interns and their eddy-bound world, for the whole eddy-bound world and the hardscrabble eddy-deprived world, what we'd done to ourselves, our children, what we'd done to our scenery, our trees, our animals, our stuffed animals!

I restrained myself no more, shooting a hand to Stoutmeier's burning back, and another to the arm of the collapsed woman. These two tensed and relaxed. For all they knew it was the hand of a helper. I saw then that we all had to join hands. Colleagues, Dignitaries, Ministers! We have to join hands! For our sake, for the animals, plants, minerals, we have to join hands and all agree at once, without rancor, with deepest self-compassion, to remove ourselves, recuse ourselves, yes, as I had done, stop ourselves, all, now, here at this teetering moment, to drink the potion, to be done. Ah to be done. The flies will rejoice. Something will be happy to feast on them. And onward. We'll feel no pain. The trees will breathe a sigh. The creatures, the ice. New intelligence will emerge, and it will start again, but it will end now. I was supine. Stoutmeier peered down. A drop of his sweat fell into my eye, blurring the round, worried face.

"You all right, chief?"

The headmistress's face appeared over Stoutmeier's, looking down with tranquil interest, as at a rare beetle.

"You two must dine at my table tonight. Promise me."

I gave a swoon. I was all right. They looked at one another and shrugged.

"Promise me."

CHAPTER TEN

IN THE BLESSED CHILL of my topmost pool I turned a somersault and watched through clear swimming goggles the galaxy of backlit bubbles wobble, scintillating, surfaceward. I sank further, back arched, limbs sprawled. Not graceful, but sensual, this pose so unthinkable in our own medium, an instant reprieved from gravity. At last I settled on my good flat float and here was something: a huge mass of vapor hunkered overhead, dense and solid-looking, cracked down the middle, a mountain-sized biscuit of the air. On either side of the crack, or chasm, were any number of ledges with cottage-like lumps where, after a perilous scramble, the denizens might gather, looking out at the civilization across the gulf, alike to theirs, inaccessible.

> Tritons,
> Reverences,
> Rotundities,
> Princes so utterly the beneficiaries of the world that I can't imagine you, even as boys with grass-stained knees, digging for a better one, who nevertheless take on this godly task, and with such gusto, when you could be fretting, rereading Moby Dick, stargazing. Oh vigorous aging men and starry upstarts,

fleet-brained devils who will depose me, depose eddy, should the world give you another ten or twenty years, which it may well, it may well . . . But perhaps what you've realized, bestriding, as you do, all of space and time, is that a few decades one way or the other, a few millennia, whether on a leafy paradise or ashen heap, comes to little enough, as in short cosmological order the whole place will be gobbled down by the exploding sun. So to be consumed by these momentary ills, to flee them so very frantically to the topmost pool of the world, yet they get in, to be so very nervous, is but a parochial, even laughable, obsessive, unhealthy way in which to discharge the sole existence, like dental flossing on death row. Perhaps if we can believe this, but really believe, in mortality, ephemerality, we might convince ourselves that all this despairing vigilance is misplaced, that we are but specks, infinitely nugatory beside the least moon in the least of the countless galaxies of countless stars burning dumbly, mechanically down the lightyears to produce for a gasp this dust of sentience, with which to see itself finally out from the mindless dark, the nebulae, my slow-falling stars, paramecia, sailfish, the pancreas, dawn, and the clouds, those fleetingest of the fleeting—we sacred chumps all the *following* existence will ever have, saving a few space aliens, one hopes, but only hopes, who in turn hope, positively pine in their own green alien hearts, that we big-headed, two-legged aliens exist somewhere, we preposterous, a billion red giant stars to each of us, in our sole care, to switch on at last with a twitch of the eyelid, and what are we looking at, what are we doing, what have we done?

Of course, we have our business, we can't all be filling the house for the universe's brief run, but would it not be sad if the house were absolutely empty, not a strange soul floating

> out there somewhere, *looking* . . . But it seems we must do something, someone must, and I'm afraid I trust the rest of you even less than I trust myself. So this. But what to say? And to you, of all people?

I selected all and deleted. The cursor drummed its thin black finger. But I was composing on the eddy, built for such crises, and it swept my attention safely off to Camera View: Zoraida's face at close range, squinting down, vexed. Screen View: *Are you sure?* appeared in a red alert box. It seemed she wasn't. The alert flowed away and eddyMessaging supervened. No new messages. Back home then, a tidy home, just one third-party app installed, or anyway the icon was far beneath eddy design standards, or really any design standard. A homespun grey square. It burst open into a plane of white surrounding the word *Now?* She must have tapped it. *Are you sure?* reappeared in its minatory red box. *Yes? Cancel?* She canceled or exited again, now to eddyCompose:

> Gratitude list: I can't. My heart is in my ears. Does it help to write this? I should have just sold out and made one close emu friend. What is it, Z? I mean, what in particular? This supposed bug of Fabio's? He's just looking for an excuse to write. Now I'm safely/unsafely gone, he's just flowing with sentiment. I think he really is worried though. For himself, or me? So now there might be a bug in the app. So now make sure there's no trail tying my tuition to the Humans. Let him know by tonight if there is one. Why tonight? What *the fuck?* I'll feel better when H gets back on this. Pretty uncharacteristic that she hasn't yet, but it's been, what, an hour? Easy, Z. Easy. Go have a sundae, a tissue stiffener—

A tissue stiffener—Wodehouse! I was only slightly relieved. I had of course understood from the first that this intern was aboard with motives other than internly, just as I was aboard with motives other than chiefly. I had put this to her credit. And I saw something of myself too in her poetic affinities, her obscure anxiety, even in the *valedictory tone*—or was I projecting? Perhaps all people are that way at some unlit depth and only my peculiar access created the illusion of peculiar likeness, or I was grasping for any ghostly company I could find. One can't put that past oneself. But now my intuition had thrown in with Wade's algorithm. It must have something to do with the summit. Of course it did. Press from the world over would be there. Protestors from the country over would be there. The famous yacht would float over all, poised for some spectacle, though I couldn't think what. Sky Yacht security—boarding procedures, detectors and so on—was severe. I searched her documents for *app*. Too much to sort through. I searched *Fabio*. Better. He had made his diary debut, in unfortunate circumstances, about a year before. The entry began:

> Since when do I notice hands? Have I stumbled into a Victorian novel? Oh those finely modeled wrists. Those workmanlike yet sensitive fingers. Intellectual cuticles. Thankfully his tube socks were in full effect or his ankles might have driven me to distraction. Let me entertain the fantasy, oh future Z, that you've actually forgotten this episode:
>
> We had gone all the way into Humans HQ to go over shit for the tenth time. Helen was late, so I was sitting in the spare room looking busy when I sensed poor Fabio hovering, I guess going over his lines. I look up, and he gets as far as the *hey, so, uh*, before freezing like a software crash, face just

stricken, sweat literally beading up on the high, intellectual forehead. And he knows. He's not going to get it out this time. You can almost see the relief.

But now I'm stricken, suddenly seeing the world as a horrendous chain of unrequitedness, and here I am another link, a functionary. Just following the rules. And here's this sweet, harmless, obviously smart, maybe in some way lovable person. Does he see the chain? Would he ever guess that this dream girl of his does it too, each time turning into the next time, trying to be cool and going off like a testimonial for Greenpeace? Not that I figured Princeton would be the best prowling ground for Miss Greenpeace Testimonial, but I guess it's getting to me, actually deranging me. And then we could feel ourself getting all Z-style anti-establishment on—what? The universe?—and then his stupid, beautiful hands: half-balled at his sides, pointer fingers making nervous figure-eights around the thumbnails. *I was no functionary*. Oh see our heroine! Very stupid, but for that one second it really was just magic, a glorious middle finger to the order. The Christmas-morning tyke look on his face before he could fix it. If I could keep that picture. Right in the midst of the crisis, the dream girl asks *him* out. But then he just nods like he's totally cool, "...all right, sometime. I mean, whenever." Right.

So God's in her heaven and all's right with the world, until I have to go through with it. Meanwhile, and this is the key, we keep catching ourself feeling *excited*, when we don't picture it too clearly, just a *kind*, fuzzily filled-in guy, a Human—okay I just groaned out loud and this girl on the train is staring at me, not dreaming that she'll be groaning out loud on the train someday. Respect the chain, girl.

This was rather more of the intern's inner life than I was looking for, or pretending not to be looking for. Not especially information-rich on the security question. Poor, deprived Zoraida. I resolved to forego further invasions. I could trust Wade's algorithm to bring up anything urgent. I would settle for *coffee*.

Emerging now from the eddy as from sleep, I saw we were flying well above the clouds. I paddled to the edge of my little pool and looked down. Rising from the undercast here and there were white, billowing masses less anxious spirits might have made extraterrestrial factory works or volcanoes. In the state I found myself, these things were not mine. They were mere clouds, weather, as they must appear to the screen-bound traveler when for a moment he looks out to check his progress across country, or to the lesser toiler who feels vaguely that the earth's furniture belongs to another, luckier race, making exceptions only for officially sanctioned beautifications like total eclipses and roadside attractions. I had two days yet. I returned to my blank document, the cursor of my mind blinking, feeling for the force that would make it move.

Over the water on my port horizon dawned a shaggy, half-grey head.

CHAPTER ELEVEN

AN INSTANT LATER A mouth clamped my shoulder, emitting one of those vibratory bellows usually reserved for baby's stomachs. This was my old acquaintance, now titled, I believe, *Director of People*. Jake had been a prince of our high school. Puffed and reddened of late, he was still snubly handsome, like an old photo you might find on Santa's bureau and ask, impressed, *is that you?* Detaching from my shoulder, he seemed on the very verge of ho-ho-ing. It was hard to credit that any more or less *compos mentis* person could be as cheery as Jake seemed. Not that he was faking it, but I suspected a desperation at the heart of his humor, an escaped convict's joyride. Maybe he after all had a more advanced sense of mortality than Wade and the rest of them. He was actually intelligent.

How was I holding up, he wanted to know. I didn't manage a response. He cocked an eyebrow. "How about that new cloud intern?"—prodding me in the side. Then addressing my groin, "you're welcome—What?" he said, drawing back, affronted. Had I said anything? "You don't think she's qualified just because she's a babe? I won't have sexism on my ship, Mr. Curtis! There's no one less than qualified here. I took a lot of care selecting these interns. You must have seen them."

This explained the peculiarities of the present crop. Jake had taken over admissions.

"The cloud girl," he was saying, "went to Princeton on scholarship before dropping out to roam Africa with one of those organizations. There's a picture of her covered in leeches I can't get out of my mind. Last year she re-enrolled and switched her major from political science to meteorology. Her essay had passages on clouds that would give you priapism."

"I appreciate it," I assured him.

I'd always thought my cloud interns were scrounged from the dregs of the general applicant pool. I'm sure the position wasn't advertised. Certainly they never seemed to know much about clouds. Zoraida had sought the cloud internship.

"I appreciate your handling all of this," I expanded. "It's unbelievable how much Wade managed to do himself for no good reason. He actually read the applications."

"To be honest," Jake said, "I had one of the interns do most of it, but I supervised like crazy. I didn't want you to be bothered with anything. I really don't mind taking on these things. We'll all have to bear up and do more now."

Jake was trying to make himself integral. Probably he too worried that without Wade he'd be jettisoned. We had picked him up at some point last year when he wrote wondering if his old friends could use a handyman or pilot-in-training. We hadn't really been friends, Jake moving in an empyrean of car exhaust and female attention that even when sitting with him in the same classroom, around the same Bunsen burner, we couldn't fully believe wasn't an invention of Hollywood. We knew from the movies what high school could be, though the likes of Jake were rarely presented. He wasn't mean or rich or a quarterback. He was a Newfoundland, a lop-eared rabbit, loping over, getting a head rub and moving on, and when he looked bored or sighed you took it as a failure of the world and snuck a mouthful of bromothymol blue to vividly drool onto the lab counter. If Wade managed to make him laugh, he was sickeningly satisfied for hours.

Jake of all people had needed our help. I never asked him about it, but the days between school and sky must have been darker ones. Maybe that's what he'd foreglimpsed even as he reveled down the locker-lined halls. Boarding the Sky Yacht, this enclosed world of weightless, student-like lives through which to tail-wag, he must have felt he'd returned at last from exile. It was a newborn I watched as he turned his chubby pink summersaults. I wouldn't lose him for the world.

"Thank you for everything," I reiterated sincerely, flicking him in the forehead, just to try it. "It does mean a lot to me."

"I know how you feel about doing the *things*," he said. "The dreaded things! The tedium!" He capsized me.

We came up spitting, elbows on the float.

"If I never told you before, Jake, I tell you now: I envy your buoyancy dearly."

"I beg your pardon," he said, surrendering the float to me.

"No no," I said.

"No," he said, and went under flailing, gasping, jetting mouth water over my leg. He grasped my rib cage and dragged me down. Even as I went thrashing under, the embrace went through me like buckshot. I hadn't been in such fleshy contact, at least with limbs I couldn't feel from both sides, in a long while, and I was almost disappointed when I had to come up to life and breathe.

"But you wanted to see me about something?" he said, easily treading water now, strings of half-greyed hair matted to the great head.

"Did I?" I said, regaining the float. Oh yes, the reports. "Is that actor still aboard, the one who read *Austerlitz*?"

"No, he's gone. Is this about *Moby Dick*?"

Months before, I had asked Jake to read *Moby Dick* for a book club I meant to start with him. As long-term inmates of a ship of sorts, I felt we might find much in Melville to discuss. I had been waiting for him to finish, or at least start.

"There are several passable recordings of *Moby Dick* already," I said with some asperity. "Do you know if we have any voice actors? Maybe one of the waitstaff?"

Jake scrolled through his mind. It was strange to think he had one, but really he did. "Too soon to say."

"Hmm . . ." I mused.

"There is a British guy."

"Fine. Can you have him report here if he isn't busy?"

"I'll have him report here *however* busy he is. Now I want to run something by you. I'm thinking, Chris, we need something new, something new to start the new era here, a catharsis, you might say."

"Yes, Jake?"

"I think a lot of us are unsure where things are going, how we fit now. I mean, from the top," he made a back and forth gesture to include the two of us, "to the interns, the staff, everyone. I want to include everyone."

"Okay."

"It may sound like a frivolous example, but do you remember at camp—"

"I didn't go to camp."

"Anyway, a lot of the interns especially are kind of idle most of the time. Unmoored is the word. There's not much *cohesion*. I'm just talking about, at bottom, team building.

Belonging, trust, unity, and of course *loyalty*." He squeezed my forearm. "Do you think it would be all right if—"

"Jake, *please*. I'm preoccupied. Consider yourself The Minister of Morale or whatever you like, and do whatever you think best. I'm not Wade. You don't have to ask me about every little thing."

"I *want* to ask you."

CHAPTER TWELVE

THROWN TOGETHER AROUND LONG, linen-clothed tables, the interns sipped cocktails, shook hands, and altogether exhibited the social fitness that had got them this far in life. All of the interns were new, most female. They looked smart, poised, unintelligible, invincible. If you didn't know how these dinners would be in only a week, you wouldn't guess they were ill at ease. I myself always felt pleasantly miniaturized in that high, glossy hall, as if ensconced in an expensive paperweight. Down below the great chandelier, a white shirt paused here or there to fill a wine glass or set down a single-malt in which, outsized and spherical, glowed a lone, lunar ice cube. I'd always enjoyed these first dinners aloft, watching the people watch each other and wonder where in all that chatter their future friend, their love, might be wondering where they were.

A waiter arrived with my nutritious smoothie. I sipped and nodded. Sympathetically, he nodded back, and out of habit filled Wade's water glass. In their innocence the staff had left a chair and place setting across from me. But in fact I had invited someone, Stoutmeier and his headmistress. I had forgotten that I, myself, would be there, or I would have asked for a third setting. Where were they? On the terrace just below mine, Executive erupted in some good-natured raillery. On the far terrace, beyond the sea of interns, sat what must have been the material incarnations of the morning's occultists, wealthy middle-aged women dressed for a night on the town. But an empty chair. No headmistress. What about Stoutmeier? No Stoutmeier either. I was a better fairy godmother than I'd imagined. I drank Wade's water and stared at the chair until the emptiness penetrated.

Was it perhaps only a misplaced awe that kept anyone from thinking to join me? Jake, seeing me up here alone, might be stirred to swoop in. I spotted the jolly fellow entertaining a table of interns out under the chandelier's farthest crystal rapids. He had put himself beside Zoraida, who looked less enchanted with him than the others did. A smile lingered neglected on her face. Her gaze, in flight, grazed mine, and once more I was back in high school, observing the lunchtime, varsity-jacketed roisterers as if by periscope from a basement broom closet. Now, in that great hall without Wade, I couldn't help feeling that Zoraida's was after all another periscope gaze, lighting on mine through the hubbub. A sundae bound for our fearsome chief counsel, Hollingsworth, with its fresh cream smell trailed one of those nostalgic flashes more vivid than real memory, as when an old song convinces you for the length of a note that once, down by the reservoir, you were a kid with a girl in your brother's car.

When I looked back, Zoraida was reabsorbed in her table, properly laughing. I finished my smoothie with a noisy aeration of the dregs.

From my balcony hammock I listened to the last bacchanalian stirrings of Jake's team-building blowout, swirling distorted and ghostly over the high dome. I was merely poking through Zoraida's files, not reading any. A folder called *Embarrassing* I passed right over. Another called *Semi-Embarrassing* contained more folders: *Essays, Moments, Poems, Possible Futures, Speeches.*

By the dozen.

Cell Biology or Ending the Penal System, The Organic Carrot and the Stick, Serfs Up or the New Feudalism, Emma Goldman Rolls in her Grave, Eulogy for the Last Polar Bear, Why We Don't Call them Robber Barons Anymore, Lucy Parsons Rolls in her Grave, Propaganda of the Deed: A Reevaluation, and, my favorite, *Out of Ordure.* Many began with *Against: Against Almonds, Against Buffalo, Against Carbon Offsets, Against eddy.*

Dated from six years ago, among the older of the collection, the teenage future cloud intern's eddy speech began:

> My friends, let's take a normal day. I'm sitting there staring at the fridge. The fridge doesn't care. I'm walking down Pine Street, getting stared at by guys at 7-Eleven. What comes next? The post office comes next. It doesn't care, and my favorite singer isn't going to come bursting out telling me how much they like my shoes today. Then where am I? Right in it—the stress, shame, boredom, loneliness. But only for a second before I'm back where I belong, where anything at all might come next, just down the scroll, or maybe someone has already sent me something, a message, a heart, *something*.
>
> We say we're feeling *dreddy*. That shouldn't be a word. I bet you've been feeling the *dredd* the whole time I've been talking. I can see you fighting it. Thank you for that courtesy. It's okay. Let's all take a look. Much better. Our world. Now look up. Worse, I agree. This world here is definitely not ours.

This one is fucked. It's someone else's. I know you adults have your hands full just getting by in it.

And us kids. We've all heard the crazy statistic. Sixteen hours a day on average down in our eddies. My generation is the first that grew up talking to emus more than real people. I won't deny it's a lot more comfortable. How I think I'm going to actually stand up in front of you all and talk like this without having a heart attack is something I still haven't figured out. Sometimes just chatting with someone between classes about their chihuahua my upper lip starts sweating. My first sexual encounter, according to the stats, isn't likely to happen till after graduation. Is that good? You parents may think so. But we look at you and you guys are lost in your eddies like any bunch of teenagers. This has to be the first time in history when pretty much all citizens, of all ages and backgrounds, are doing the same thing all day, everywhere.

Friends, we have been *standardized*.

Why? I wonder who on earth benefits from us all spending our waking lives totally accounted for, in a highly controlled version of reality. I wonder what's sliding by while we're all feeding away, expressing ourselves, huffing and puffing, setting those other people straight. Unfortunately they're real, right, those deluded suckers who cause so much trouble? Are they? Are you? It's our world, for sure, but someone else is making it, someone who knows us very well. Well enough to *make us*. Your ex is probably yelling at some version of you right now. You gave yourself to him, to her, to eddy, for nothing.

But eddy are the good guys, right? At least neutral. All hail Wade Aubrey, holy saint of grace and efficiency, literally floating over our heads right now. Except not *right now*, or we'd all run out and take a Sky Yacht selfie. I've done that!

I think about that all the time. That's it, little doggies. Step right up and smile with the flagship of inequality. Get your good angles.

This is not a commons, this world in your hand. It's capital. It's exactly what's decimated the world they don't want us to look around at. It's what decides which wars we fight, who lives, who dies. That's who decides what you see and what you do all day. It's capital controlling you just like always, and like never before. *Sixteen* hours. They got you at work. Then they got you in your living room. Now they just got you. The illusion of freedom is finally complete.

Yes, I'll take one question.

The lady wants to know what I'm proposing to do about it. I haven't come up with a concrete plan yet, but it has to start with de-standardizing ourselves. Give that emu generator program a meltdown. Make your ex berate some totally unsatisfactory version of you. I'm not saying go around in a kilt with an albino rat on your shoulder, but look at the things other people aren't seeing. That's not hard right now. Talk to a celebrity all your friends aren't talking to. Or just go cold-turkey. Get past that dredd. Find your thing. Find out who you would have been if eddy and the apps hadn't driven you into their ready-made channels. Being a weirdo is no longer a non-political position. The survival of the planet basically depends on you being the amazing, particular weirdo they don't want you to know that you are.

Don't squander that. I almost did, as you've probably heard. I tried to off myself. Me too. I guess this isn't news. Well now I'm up here being the weirdo, trying to do something, and I can tell you it feels a lot better. I guess that's my tentative answer. I want to see more weirdos.

I switched to Camera View as though to see the writer in the angst of her teenage room, dropping back moist-eyed to catch an ovation from the future. What I got instead was the neon-outlined skylights of another future, dance music, Jake's unintelligible voice, now a bare-legged giant stepping over, checking her eddy on a neighboring beach chair. The orgy Jake had gotten together under the banner of team building was still underway, it seemed, in the lower pool. I switched back to Zoraida's anti-eddy screed. It was unnerving, offensive, and rather moving. The poor fantasy of it, of feeling better. Had she at the time of writing already tried to *off* herself, or was this too part of the fantasy, a projection? Had she since?

A projection, or fantasy: our Zoraida had not been the most well-adjusted soul. She hated, blamed eddy. She had gotten herself up here to off the sainted Wade Aubrey. And now she would have to settle for me. A shiver of something, not terror, not quite terror, trilled my spine. I had never been the sort to think with serious intent, much less titillation, about taking my own life, but some more qualified person handling the job was a new consideration. I couldn't deny a flutter. To be taken off one's own hands, without effort or responsibility. Courageous wasn't the word, but how gracefully would you fall from the sky? From so light a life, yet in the end even this one, like any, more or less heavy? To go down there after all this time and *get a life*—so self-evidently futile the phrase was used only as insulting hyperbole, never wished on a friend.

Friends,
Officers,
Conquerors,
Let's take a normal day. We're gazing at the sunset. Lava

traces undersides and flows along, revealing unsuspected contours, of the same clouds, of different clouds, until an encampment of high grey strokes we had given up for lost is suddenly the lone pink faithful of the sky. These unlikely second acts. Yes, we are feeling dreddy. Why shouldn't that be a word? When, I'd like to know, weren't we? There was one year, maybe two. The more embalmed of you world-shakers will remember that only three decades ago and for all the millennia before, we had nowhere, simply nowhere but in our own cramped insides to stuff the sharers of our sunsets, our smiles, all those phantoms we carried along to mop up the moments too big, too poignant, to compass alone. Our suns rose and we made our wistful broadcasts—look, you lot, *look*, the leaves, *listen*—this was imagination, reflex. Then we in this room, we sorcerers, snatched the audiences from all those inner theaters and stuck them directly, miraculously into life. There they were, the real ones, watching, listening, at our instant disposal. All that unbearable fleeting time, the weight of it, taken up, spread over solid human shoulders! But would they look, the real ones? As it turned out, yes. Surprisingly. Constantly. More than that, they would *applaud*. Can you remember, today, the first time this happened, that feeling, the lightness? And what did I do? I added only the bygone, the lost, dragged them close enough anyway for the fallible heart, talking, *listening* again.

What miracles, gentlemen, can't we curdle!

We realize rabid dreams. We vault over doubt. Others catastrophize. We create. Had our morbid imaginations been fully developed, we wouldn't be here in this lavish hall, in

> this blasted world. Dauntlessness, drive, a sense of possibility, these manias had their place. No longer. We must be rehabilitated, replaced. By whom? In our greatness we didn't overlook providing our own saviors: those who have known only our world, our successes, the squeezed, the limited, the daunted, gentlemen, the young! Now permit me to introduce my own replacement, the doubting, the benighted...

Again I tried Camera View. We were in a pocket, or she had someone in the dark with her. A conversation was clearly audible.

"Here it is," came Zoraida's high voice.

"What are you actually trying to do to me?" came another.

I recognized it as that of our young COO, Morgan Palmer. Palmer's eddy then, Camera View: dimly lit, close together, and naked at least from mid-chest up, Palmer and Zoraida stared out at me, at the screen. Screen View: a repeating loop recorded at the main pool. Pale young people in swimsuits cheered, clapping bare stomachs with the hand not holding a bright plastic cup. They were roughly congealed according to swim cap color: fuchsia, blue, signal green, and mauve. Four likewise colored flags bearing attempts at heraldic crests drooped from pool-skimming poles at each of the four corners. On the lifeguard chair above all swayed old Jake, red-faced, gesticulating, ecstatic. This was team building. A few rungs down, holding the ladder with one hand, Stoutmeier inspected a shot on the back of a big, professional camera, and took aim at something in the water.

Whoever had *posted* this footage followed his lead, pushing between two bare backs to reveal the main pool, a laned, pedantic thing. The action was a relay race. A woman in mauve swim cap and clashing red two-piece thrashed a valiant pseudo-breaststroke as a muscled, green-capped man sailed into frame a lane over. I was surprised that Palmer, the man could be none other, had deigned to participate, but after all he was very young for a COO, probably not averse to surveying Jake's new crop of interns in their April pallor, and clearly a swimmer. He was poised to glide past poor, thrashing Zoraida like an eel—no doubt he had grown up with a pool, had attended schools with pools—when the intern broke off, slid under the lane divider, and seized the oncoming COO with arms and legs. By the time he registered the attack, she had him from behind in a headlock. The angle zoomed up and caught Zoraida's face, fierce and earless. The two sank under.

"How do you know you're not going to kill me?" demanded Palmer, back on Camera View in the present.

"What makes you think I wasn't trying to?"

"*Nothing*," said the COO, rubbing his muscular neck. Water frothed at their shoulders. They were in a luxurious bathroom, every bit as big as my own, ensconced in a jacuzzi tub. I didn't have a jacuzzi tub.

"Is that why you're here?" Palmer asked.

"Maybe."

For an instant, real jealousy clutched me.

"I'm saving this as evidence," Palmer said, tapping the screen.

"Wait, what was that?" Zoraida pulled his hand back. "Writing? An original Morgan Palmer?"

"Go ahead," Palmer said. "God knows no one else is going to see it."

"This is the eddy talk," Zoraida observed, confused. "You're giving it?"

Palmer scoffed. "I thought I might get the chance. But your boy Mr. Curtis is coming down from his cloud for the occasion. Now understand, this is a man who . . ." Palmer proceeded to bemoan himself with remarkable freedom on the subject, his lovely green eyes at one point filling with the injustice of my taking over the talk. On-screen, the speech scrolled and scrolled.

I tossed my eddy to the foot of the hammock. Already blue had seeped in above my vigil. Was I the only one in the place not bursting at the seams with speeches? Palmer should give the eddy talk. Zoraida should give the eddy talk. Suppose I really did appoint her Wade's successor? There in my balcony bubble, in the vanishing stars, I resolved to at least keep her from harm, from jail, from whatever it was, her own young spirit. I resolved to get dressed.

CHAPTER THIRTEEN

WHEN AT LAST THE stair door clicked, I jumped. But it was a waitress under a heavy tray. This young woman, indistinguishable by sight from one of the present crop of interns, swung open a stand and laid out the breakfast I had ordered. Rattling off some description, the girl plucked up pewter domes, exposing the foodstuff. The coffee had been roasted in a certain way, and there was an eloquent passage about the brewing process. She went. The sky was overcast and undercast. The yacht drifted down between until it rested like a Faberge egg on the lower cloud shelf. Then we dropped through the whiteout to catch the first of what would be three diminishing sunrises if Goldfarb properly timed our ascent.

Zoraida appeared as we rose with the sun back through the lower whorl. Despite her late-night soak and whatever followed, she looked fresh. Only her clothes, an itchy-looking grey dress just this side of tweed, showed creases. She wore new sunglasses.

"Madame," I said, attempting jovial, lifting a pewter dome.

"No, you go ahead," she deferred. "I had a little something."

"No you didn't."

"Well, take half. You look like you had a rough night."

"Zoraida," I said severely, "eat." The girl's ribs in that pool had looked awfully distinct. A few months on the Sky Yacht would do her good.

She hesitated. "Do you mind? For my mom."

She wanted to take a picture, or as it turned out a video, opening with a shot of French toast aslant on the china, the juice like a column of sun, and up the gradient to the pinking country of the upper shelf. Some eddy hater this was.

"Let me ask you something," I embarked once she had a good mouthful in process. I was still choosing from the dozen inadequate openings I'd contemplated, when, moved by some demon, the headmistress, breaking off from her invariable circuit, flowed our way, eyes wide, seeing. She glided to a halt unsociably close. I could smell licorice, or probably fennel. The intern's head reeled back in an *excuse you*. Despite the sage's poreless skin, she looked older standing beside the intern. Or rather it was that Zoraida looked younger beside her, less formidable, less formed.

"Excuse me," the headmistress responded to Zoraida's gesture with magisterial disinterest, the words merely a curtain she yanked down between them before addressing herself to me. "I'm sorry, but it's unacceptable what's happening here."

"No, she's my—"

"We'd like to be let off at the next town. My students did not sign on for Fort Lauderdale spring break."

"Oh that was just a team-building exercise, to establish cohesion and so on."

"I heard explosions at three a.m. On a blimp."

"It did run late. I apologize."

If this complaint reached the board, it would be held

hard against the yacht's already tenuous future. Wade had warranted any indulgence, including that of myself. I did not.

"My course," the headmistress pursued, "depends on the establishment of a safe space. This space used to be safe. I understand things didn't go as planned. I'm sorry. I'm just asking to be evacuated. Should I be talking to you about this? Should I be talking to someone else?"

"No, me," I said eagerly. "I'll speak to Goldfarb about getting you down. He's the pilot, Goldfarb."

"Speak to Goldfarb."

"Yeah," Zoraida added. "You can't be violating safe spaces right and left just because there's been a company tragedy and everyone wants to get past it for one night and figure out how to move forward together. Hey, I saw plenty of your disciples at the pool last night. That one heiress lady was putting the rest of us to shame. It was probably her setting off the firecrackers. Do you know how hard it is to actually jeopardize our safety here? If your heiress had a heap of dynamite and years to plan it, she couldn't take the Sky Yacht down, believe me. And here's Mr. Curtis, who wasn't even there, just trying to survive total personal and professional collapse. Are you going to tell me you don't see him sipping his little smoothie all alone at that table? Do you know what my whole job is? As far as I can tell, it's to keep this poor sack company while he looks at the clouds for hours on end trying not to jump overboard—"

"Hey," I said.

"Do you really have to be some kind of priestess in a nightgown to see that this man is in rough shape?"

"Zoraida."

"Or does he only become visible after paying you to teach him how to care about other people?"

The headmistress eyed the intern as one might a child mid-supermarket-tantrum, and now me, the delinquent parent. I was of course embarrassed to be discussed this way, embarrassed over Zoraida, and proud of her. I said palliatively:

"We can fly you down when we stop for the summit, tomorrow night I think it is, if that's an acceptable delay. And I'll gladly refund you, for last session as well."

"*What?*" said Zoraida.

"That's very generous," the headmistress acknowledged. "Thank you."

She floated off.

"Bitch," said Zoraida into her orange juice. "Earth-body *was* a good idea, and she just couldn't help turning it into a finishing school, lulling these rich people who could actually make a difference into thinking they have time to restore themselves before they can bring that energy to the earth. Doctor, heal thyself. Too late." She shook her head at the horizon. "Too goddamn late."

"She's an interesting specimen," I suggested. "She makes this circuit every sunrise in a transport of self-sufficiency. She doesn't even look. No one sees this but me."

"What, you like her?" Zoraida turned a squint on me.

"She doesn't even look. But speaking of the summit," I followed quickly. "What do you predict will happen?"

Still holding me in her squint, Zoraida set down the juice. "You're giving the big commercial-constitution, save-the-world speech. You're for Egarp, right? Or did Wade Aubrey have something up his sleeve like all these people are fantasizing?"

"Suppose he did. What would you suspect it is?"

"Search me," she said.

"Yes," I said, coughing. "I mean to say, what sort of thing do you think would really make an . . . impact?"

"As in," she said, "what would I say to all those leaders if I were you?"

This wasn't what I was aiming at, but what would she say to all those leaders if she were me?

"Yes," I said, excited, "what would you say?"

"You really want to know?" She smiled, sweetly.

"Very much."

She put her fingers in her ears and sang "la la la la la." She removed her fingers, sweetly smiling.

That was what she thought I should say.

"The other constitution . . . Egal?" I suggested. "Or that Green Road business?"

"Flip a coin," she said.

Something better, something better for these doomed young people. She had no faith in the summit, of course, or none anyway in the official program.

"Tell me . . ." I approached from another side, "what was it that drew you to meteorology?"

For her purposes, whatever they were, it had to be better, and far quicker, than studying graduate-level business management or whatever the proper interns had to endure to get aboard.

She hiked her slight shoulders. "I care about the planet. And it's called climate science."

"I care about the planet," I said brightly.

"Okay."

"The planet is *stupendous*," I enlarged. "Even the least part of it, I mean, if you *look*."

"I agree, Mr. Curtis, but I can't not point out that you haven't glanced at the planet since I've been here."

"Well, maybe not the planet per se . . ."

She looked much as Palmer did when dealing with me, a contained, semi-stunned forbearance. I was annoying. Well, I may not have looked at the *ground* first thing in the morning, but at night, the colored lights of some unknown city suffusing the overcast with tantalizing potentials . . . And I did thoroughly approve of the oceans, certain mountain ranges, trees, individually and in clumps, great flocks of leaves in gentle or violent sway. Even the cities I liked. But I recalled, back when we were still quartered in so-called Silicon Alley, those commutes when the subway at last swooped out over the East River and the preposterous dreamscape of lower Manhattan, with, often as not, glowering from Downtown to the archway of the Bayonne Bridge, a vaster Manhattan of the air, roiled and glowing, unseen by my fellow riders, prostrate to other glows, or standing dully at the doors, always in-facing, blocking the windows like bouncers to wonder itself. And it wasn't true that I never looked down, sometimes in broad day, at the wilderness, cattle, Utah. We had never gone far enough to see ice flows or the aurora borealis, but maybe now, after the summit.

"Is it that you love the planet just so much you can't bear to see it in this state?" she said.

The question didn't seem quite sincere. At *can't bear to see it in this state*, an unbeckoned vision rose from that first-rate facility down there, with its kind, competent nursing staff.

"I have to make a call," I said.

"In that case, I can catch breakfast with the others. You eat the rest of this. You don't look good."

As I watched her go, I tried and succeeded in not absurdly falling in love with her in lieu of the departing headmistress.

I walked a little way around the bow, where I wouldn't smell the French toast. Waiting for my father's emu to pick up, I looked over the whole of the sky. It seemed she had at least succeeded in curtailing the squeegee bots. I hadn't seen one since early afternoon of the day before.

CHAPTER FOURTEEN

WE PIERCED THE PLUMP belly of a cumulus, a moment you can never convince yourself won't come with a satisfying pop, and I thought of Stoutmeier. For his sake too I was sorry our headmistress was leaving. Unless things had gone badly with them the previous night. I had neglected to snoop. Camera View now revealed the man looming over a desk, shirtless, writing with absorption. A love note? He paused, reviewed the page, smirked, glistened, stroked the grey stubble. I was switching to Screen View when a security alert swooped in with special urgency. Beeping and without asking my leave, it presented a text conversation even then in progress between Palmer and someone titled Interim Director of Physical Security.

> **Palmer:** Obvious bullshit, straight from the administration. They're trying to keep us from going over their heads at the summit and getting the smart constitution ratified. If we weren't already suing, I'm sure they would just ground us again. They clearly don't have the evidence.
>
> **IDPS:** Yeah, pretty desperate move on their part.

Palmer: I guess they haven't heard that the eddy presentation will be given by our resident *visionary*, and we're just as likely to propose a weekly world-wide snow day in honor of the morning star.

IDPS: Ha

Palmer: In your professional experience, does this so-called threat strike you as even remotely legitimate?

IDPS: Not from what little they've given me. I still have to counsel we land.

Palmer: Appreciated, but didn't Homeland admit after Nevada that there are no domestic groups with long-range missile capability? Aren't we completely secure from onboard attacks? Am I missing something?

IDPS: Yeah it's not possible to hit the gas bladders from the passenger compartment with the amount of explosive that could be accumulated from onboard supplies. The one documented vulnerability is if such an explosive is flown to the gas through an emergency exit, but that would involve making a drone from scratch out of onboard supplies, and really four drones from scratch. We can stay up long enough to evacuate even if three of the five bladders go. Wade couldn't figure out how to make even one drone from onboard supplies. He just refused to rule it out. And all the exits are monitored.

Palmer: Okay. Thanks again, Homeland. Over and out.

IDPS: I have to counsel...

Palmer: Counsel noted.

IDPS: Just to cover my ass, should I escalate to Curtis?

Palmer: Ha. Good luck with that.

IDPS: Noted :)

I wasn't so confident. It's true acts of major domestic terrorism even back then were volcanically rare—Sky-Yacht-scale incidents came perhaps once in a generation; they very much defined a generation—and we had just, months before, responded to our first serious threat in a decade, as it turned out, bogus. Our chief counsel Hollingsworth, incensed to highest Hollingsworth bullfrogdom—you might have popped him with a felt pen to the neck—filed a suit against Homeland Security or whoever it was down there in Nevada making things hard for us the way we had made things hard for them with our privacy measures, our refusals, before deciding their intelligence after all had been faulty, further analysis revealing no radical domestic group training long-range missiles at us, as of course they weren't. Three weeks went by before they would let us beyond their perimeter—armed vehicles, troops—as though the surrounding desert, stretching flat to the horizon without the threat of so much as a cactus prick, were teeming with camouflaged militias. Not that the place wasn't teeming with camouflaged militias, but I think those were on the whole woodsier phenomena, or at least suburban. What bothered me most was that not a day's drive off in Arizona the great James Turrell earthwork, which, after decades spent connecting open-sky sanctuaries with tunnels aligned to biannually sun-strike one after another waiting obelisk, had opened around then, and I still hadn't seen it, though from our imprisonment, on clear days, I could almost make out the spot with my telescope. The colonel in charge— how such a person came to be in charge of natural formations like Hollingsworth and Palmer, not to mention poor Wade, really took one back to the world wars—would listen patiently enough to my pleas. Anyway, it all came to nothing.

Now I was not so convinced that whoever it was hadn't received some tip, but suspected it was to do with Zoraida's designs on my life. I was just checking in on her when another security alert sounded. It was a brief letter just arrived in the Interim Director of Physical Security's spam folder:

> I'm sure you won't see this but I have to try it, I already tried Homeland Security. I work with a group called the Humans, don't bother looking it up. We have some funding though and happen to have an incredibly deep and original mind (not mine), which I don't want to see harmed. I don't want to see anyone harmed actually and right now I can't say that you all on the Sky Yacht will be safe if you go to the summit. I can't give more information without compromising someone, I'm just sending up a prayer that you can sense I'm not crazy and will please please get everyone off before you reach the summit. If you won't stop your whole thing just because of some guy writing to you with almost no information, I understand and just beg you to at least offload the interns, who are not even getting paid to expose themself to these kinds of risks. If nothing happens, what do you lose? I'm

sorry I ever got involved in this. I've tried to do something to reduce the odds, but unfortunately that also involves people listening to me.

    P.S. Don't waste your time trying to trace this message, I'm a software engineer.

Software engineer . . . My mind went to the mysterious, buggy app, the *Are you sure?* in its minatory red alert box. I even remembered the name Fabio, app developer Fabio of the perfect, nervous hands, who was so worried about Zoraida, who had worried her, this from the diary, to let him know if there was anything on paper connecting her with the Humans. The deep mind, surely, was hers. And yet, surely, it didn't intend casualties far beyond myself. Camera View revealed a bare ceiling. But there was a fresh addition to her journal.

> Anxiety dreams at all-time highs. From today's pitiful nap attempt, my berth was the back seat of the old car. He wasn't driving, no one was. Delicate little bursts flew by the windows, a school of fish or stars. I was desperate to get out, but I knew if I opened the door water would come rushing in, or all the air would rush into space.
>
> I just called emu dad and finally asked if he remembered driving me to the fireflies. I could face his not remembering, and it would have been a pity not to talk about it once. Of course he didn't remember.
>
> My mind feels squeezed down to a walnut, and I don't know what I can say to soothe it here. I'm almost looking forward to

awkward sunset with Mr. C. A little quiet . . . *like a torn cloud before the hurricane.*

"Dilworth?"

"Yeah?"

"Kindly have my intern meet me on deck at once. There's a cloud formation on which I would like her opinion."

It would have been nice, if only for the sake of verisimilitude, had there been a cloud formation, or even a cloud, in sight. I might have made do with a lake, but below were only the usual forested hills like the backs of green sheep nosing north, sheered here and there by some beetle infestation or fire. The stair door clicked, and I fixed my gaze on the horizon. How to get her out of whatever it was she'd got herself into?

"You know," I said casually, as if merely in continuation of the silence, "every day I talk to an emu of my father."

"Really?"

The tone, I was sorry to note, was less that of a companion in this melancholy practice than of a competent babysitter.

"Yes," I affirmed.

For a long while we faced the sky.

"I find it relieving," I added.

"How recent was it?"

"Every day."

"I mean, when did he pass?"

"He didn't."

"Oh," she said. "Oh."

"And your own father?" I persevered.

"He died."

"And do you ever talk to his emu?"

I looked at her, kindly.

"I do appreciate your product," she offered. "I'm sure millions of people are grateful to talk to their passed relatives. Thank you."

"No, no. I mean were you close?"

"He was in and out."

"What did he do?"

"Hustled. What he could."

"Successfully?"

She shrugged. "He had a beautiful car."

She had dreamed about this car today. How to use this?

"The car . . ." I ventured.

She looked around the deck for help, maybe the headmistress with another noise complaint.

"He would swing by in it sometimes and take you somewhere?" I elaborated.

I was aiming for the fireflies which she had apparently longed to discuss. I wanted to hear about these fireflies. I felt I would understand the fireflies.

"It was just this gorgeous old car he must have bought sometime when his ship came in. In the end, he was sleeping in it. It made noise, you couldn't go over forty, but it looked good. It looked *rich.* All leather and shiny chestnut or oak, or whatever they use. And it was smooth. Riding around you didn't feel the road. It was like floating."

"The Ground Yacht."

"Yeah." And she repeated in an eerie undertone, "The ground yacht."

Fireflies, however, did not follow. Again we gazed off in our accustomed awkwardness. I looked at my hands. My index fingers traced nervous patterns on my thumbnails, which badly wanted cutting, and cleaning. Far from perfection. I pocketed them.

"I want to thank you," I resorted to her preferred subject matter, "for wrangling those infamous squeegee bots. I've hardly seen any of late. You must have got them rounded up? Reprogrammed?"

"You could say that," she said, although with less self-congratulation than she had a right to. The things were menaces.

In fact, far from self-delight, through her eyes seemed to streak, like one of those figmenty falling stars you need someone else to confirm as real, a chill, something anyway, which an instant later I couldn't swear to having seen, but then if any of us are geniuses with other people, as my father's emu would have it, we're all geniuses with other people in one way, that is, that it's not by the dramatic, juicy arrangement of events—catching our beloved in the act, the lipstick stain, or even the faintest whiff of perfume—that we discover we know, but by indications so subtle we struggle to bring them out as evidence. It was something in the tone, the timing, the minuscule muscle aside the eye, some subliminal diversion from the millennia-engrained social protocol that the part of ourself that is the genius with other people, and always the genius of bad news, picks up and reports back to our clunking consciousness, which might have stood waiting another decade for a hair on the brush: Something is amiss. And what's amiss is exactly what we knew it was. Before deciding we're being ridiculous.

I was being ridiculous, but I could not right myself in the moment. I don't know what my own face might have given Zoraida just then. I hardly saw her. Beyond, over the great clear dome, spots seemed to swarm like an army of squeegee bots. The sky dimmed, and through the dark scrolled *the one vulnerability . . . four drones from scratch . . . all the exits are monitored.*

"What's wrong?" Zoraida said. "Hey, hey," she tapped my hand, alarmed. "Have you had anything to eat today? Here, sit down, sit with me for a second." She sat me down against the transparent rail. "I'm going to get you some water. I'll be right back. Okay?"

"Yes, I'm sorry. Thank you."

CHAPTER FIFTEEN

WHEN SHE'D PASSED INTO the starboard stairs, I got myself up and eventually to my office. In her documents, *Humans* abounded. Here indeed was one called *The Humans App.* The app. But apparently it abbreviated the other kind of application, for which one might write a five-page essay draft, beginning:

> Sane, sensible people recognize their life as a gift. Cherish it, protect it, until you create another one to cherish and protect, and so on indefinitely. The greatest threat is the threat to our indefiniteness. The greatest tragedy is to lose it partway, even three-quarters. The value of those lost years of life is inestimable. But let's be crude. What does one half of a big, flabby, tepid, protected life go for? What's the exchange in lean, hot, unprotected lives? What is our great gift worth on the global market, everything done right, the best deal we can broker? More than half a life? A lot more? We know the answer. And yet, are we really having such a good time here? If we were, would we deserve it? I see anesthetized people, not happy ones.

Rather a truculent opening for an application essay. What followed was less supplication than manifesto. The *anesthesiologists* were, unsurprisingly, the tech companies which had bought and sold the general consciousness, "the headsmen and undertakers of individuality and democracy, the terminal illusionists." A strike at the heart of them, where they lived, the ubiquitous, invincible, sainted mother of them all, the medium itself—eddy—might raise the first world's "perma-inclined head" for long enough to thrust us momentarily back into unmediated, unbearable existence. Relieved from control—the left, the right, the lesser, niche narratives of the day—people might once more become individuals, seeing and acting in their own environment, restored to agency, compassion, intelligence, the healthy neurons of a healthy societal brain. A functioning civilization could emerge only from functioning individuals. Control from above had failed every time, and finally.

Eddy's luxury yacht literally floating above the plutocratic parliament and its fascistic armed defenders must not be passed up. The serene unconcern of the robber barons, whom "it would never even cross our minds to call robber barons anymore, so complete is their conquest of our psyche," would be burst along with the hypnosis they perpetrated on their subjects.

One *individual* could do this, but who? Another angry man? The explosive act would be at once dismissible. Even sophisticated, articulate men faired poorly here. Alexander Berkman's act of supreme self-sacrifice was met with scorn, even by the workers for whom he gave his freedom. A woman, on the other hand, this novelty the media runs with. If, according to ridiculous, heteronormative beauty standards, she's an attractive one, it runs that much farther and more giddily. Lucy Parsons, against all racial odds. Patriarchy's long insistence on the meekness and objecthood of woman paradoxically legitimized these messages of strength. Berkman's female partner and co-conspirator had the world's ear for decades. Now Emma Goldman is hardly known. Yet a return to Gilded Age inequality called for a return of the Emmas and Lucys, a return of their weapon of choice.

Which, my eddy informed me, was dynamite.

The anxiety with which I awaited Zoraida so scuttled sunset it was almost a relief when at last she appeared, greatly shrunken to the size and shape of a girl in jeans and a checked blouse. Approaching, she gave a quick, awkward wave from the hip and took up her post beside me at the rail, leaning out, westward. Whatever those eyes might have made of it, for an instant their companionship got the better of me, and I observed that a mob of low, grey clouds formed a spectral gallery, some space above which, like flaming justices, sat a row of huge pink cumuli.

The cloud intern exhaled in seeming appreciation. "I am glad I got to see this," she said, and nodded to herself, confirming.

I struggled to take this as the calculated dissimulation of a devil. To the ear, before post-processing, it sounded more the old valedictory note. I stole a square look at the girl, leaning out over the clouds, the sunglasses, on which I had insisted, raised in compromise on the short, chaotic tufts, the new blouse rolled up to the slight elbows, this waif. I couldn't see it. Even then, feeling the wounded righteousness of the duped, all that interest in the squeegee bots which in my innocence I had taken for enthusiasm, the hand-wringing about the emergency evacuation procedures for which my fatuous heart had gone out to her, still I couldn't see it.

No, if at that moment squeegee bots were clinging with explosive charges underside the gas bladders, awaiting only a signal from the fateful app, it wasn't for her own safety she had been worried. This was a sensitive, sensible, deeply unhappy person. Watching her so absorbed in the clouds from the fastness of her own worries, this fellow stowaway, I even felt some pity that her plan, so long dreamed and marvelously carried from benighted conviction to execution, would come to nothing. The squeegee bots! Wade always said that no human-created system is without a bug, almost always a surprisingly big one, and Zoraida had found it, had outsmarted—but for his cheating with the security app—the great savant himself. I wanted to generate a proper emu of Wade just to tell him. And by an intern. No, it wasn't herself she feared wouldn't make it off in time. How much time? Hadn't that security fellow said something about staying aloft a few minutes even if three of the gas bladders go? She must have planned to take out only three, at least until the place was evacuated. I would bet on it.

"Hello," I said, annoyed, into my eddy. "I'm sorry, but sunset is in progress, a particularly critical phase of pink just now. If I could perhaps call you back after . . . I appreciate that, but surely . . ."

I paused, listening.

"No," I said. "Absolutely not. We're not landing. Yes, that's final, official, what have you . . . Well, if you must, come find me here after sunset. Yes, thank you." I hung up.

Zoraida looked at me.

"Oh, it's nothing," I said, irritated. "It seems one of the gas bladders has been leaking. It happens. It really makes no difference. Better not to tell anyone though."

She looked concerned, but then she would have to look concerned.

"It's all right," I said, as if to comfort. "We can stay aloft just fine with one gas bladder out. Even with two. The place was carefully designed with so-called *redundancy*. The only issue, which isn't a real issue, is that if by some absurd coincidence three of the other bladders happen to lose their gas, and for that matter very quickly—essentially if all three go up in flames—then it's bad. With three bladders out, we have a few minutes to evacuate. With four, we crash."

"Do you know which, which gas bladder?" Her eyes simulated innocent fear, but she wanted to know. Was it one of her three, or a fatal fourth?

"That I don't," I said. "But I see I've alarmed you. I shouldn't have said anything. Forget it."

She produced a relieved smile, but color told in her temple and cheek. Or it was the reflected deepening of the sky. She returned to the horizon, so that I couldn't see her face. I thought I made out a sharp intake of breath, but it might have been a sniff. People sniff. I was not so practiced at these tricks to be confident. I had never before in my life faked a call, at least in the non-emu sense. She could of course have no inkling that I knew; it would not occur to her that I was bluffing, and now the poor thing was obliged to stand there admiring the hues as if, along with the purported gas, the last year or more of her young life hadn't just leaked away, all that ingenuity and care, that fledgling self-assurance and anticipation. I wanted to tell her it would be all right, she would be all right, that some older, adjusted, equanimous self would thank her stars for this setback, this snuffing. And I wanted to give her something, a surrogate, something for the moment. She would take it, for just as I caught myself imagining I wasn't finished on the Sky Yacht, so too she would imagine she wasn't, somehow, and being younger and more spirited, her denial would be that much more robust than mine. She would find her hopes oozing off into a new course, if I could only provide one, a course her reason might, in better conditions, reject. As with matter and energy, a law of conservation applied. Our hope twists, transmutes, writhes, but doesn't vanish. We are, sadly, such creatures.

Catching the set sun, a contrail cut a pale pink slice in the sky. Officials en route to the summit.

"We'll be stopping for the summit tomorrow," I remarked bluffly, pressing a ragged thumbnail into my forefinger, "which reminds me I have an urgent duty to impose on you."

She quarter-turned my way. The quarter view looked merely curious.

"This is where you really earn your money as my intern. I'll be giving the eddy talk after all, as you may have heard."

She betrayed no sign of having been wept on by Palmer over this.

"Anyway, I've been working up some notes, but generally I don't write my own talks . . ." I flapped an effete, explanatory hand at the horizon. "If I could just ask you to do a little speechwriting . . . Do you have any experience with that? Have you ever written a speech?"

"Once or twice," she said.

"Good," I said. "Splendid."

I wanted her to believe she had a certain latitude in forming the address, that the vague, spoiled, disinterested Chris Curtis might parrot most anything. Parroting most anything wasn't so far from my hopes. Here was one with the properly developed morbid imagination, sure to turn out some insightful material—raw material. Anything was better than the blank page, that gloating cursor. But beyond this undignified hope was a fear that without any other avenue she might see her way back to her scheme, so nearly done, still in a sense viable, maybe even ennobled. Healthy, upstanding people, generals and so on, make such calculated decisions with human life right and left. One need only believe madly enough in one's own conceptions, and be firm. One could almost imagine firmness.

"Come down to the office," I said, "and I'll give you the reports from the other delegates, as well as our own, if you'd like to read those for background. I imagine you're fairly well up on policy, but if it would be interesting."

Her face remained impassive, though such an activist, anarchist, whatever she was, couldn't sneer at privileged access to the great, secret doings of the world-movers. At length, the brow screwed up, though whether with incredulity or disgust I couldn't say—I had lost the common genius of subtle perception. It was all I could do to keep track of my own parts.

"Aren't those kind of a big deal?" she asked.

"Quite," I affirmed.

"I mean, security-wise? I've looked for them online before. They're never even leaked. Should you really be giving that stuff to your intern?"

"Well, if you're interested," I said. "And if you want me to give you some direction, but I'm sure you have a sense of what I'd say by now. I'm up on the second, possibly third, day, so I'd appreciate if you got started."

Yes, with a little massaging of the raw matter, a little toning down . . .

"I'm not sure I do have a sense of what you'd say," she said.

"Just write something. I don't want to think about it anymore."

"Just write whatever?"

"Yes, yes, but please hurry. And of course don't tell anyone."

She peered into me as if to assure herself I really was this vacuous, really so precisely what she'd expect. I imagine she came up with a positive, yet she didn't seem pleased. She didn't seem heartbroken either. Perhaps she was, above all, relieved, this principled, sky-appreciating, misguided girl, that through no fault of her own the enormity, the pressure, the great risk she had put herself up for, had been lifted from her shoulders. Unless it had been pressed down harder.

"I am sorry to put this on you," I said, "but I've gotten a bit behind . . . It's been a difficult couple of weeks."

"Would it make more sense to have someone else give the talk, or at least write it?" she asked reasonably.

"Who?"

"One of the other executives, I don't know. Morgan Palmer maybe, or someone?"

"Oh I couldn't stick Palmer with this so late in the day. Now please, don't worry about it. You interns are chosen with great care for this sort of thing. I'm sure you'll do wonderfully."

"Right."

She was getting herself through the minutes of dealing with me.

"Okay," she said, dutifully taking out her eddy. "What do you want to say?"

"To say . . . ?"

She waited, poised.

"Oh I don't know. Just write what you think is good."

"What I think is good is probably not what you think."

"Enough," I said. "Here, I'll make a contract. Eddy, take note. I, Christopher Curtis, agree to speak at the confounded summit whatever my intern Zoraida Simpson prepares for me, without any limitations or conditions, except that: a. she bothers me no more about it; b. she tells no one, except as it may be necessary to produce this contract in a legal proceeding against me. Signed, etc."

"Are you all right?"

"Yes. It's just that my life has taken rather a turn, and at this point I simply can't deal with summits and the fate of the millions. I'm sure the feeling is mutual. What do I know? What does even Palmer know? We executives, you understand, get caught up in our immediate interests, entrenched ideas, so on, and lose sight of the real market, the real needs. You yourself would have a better notion than I these days what would be good for the average eddy customer, the young people especially. If we lose you, we're finished—some agile young startup takes our place, like we did to the others back in our day. Eddy is the institution now, the dinosaur. We're ossifying. Look at me. I'm ossifying by the second. And this talk of course goes beyond eddy. You know the situation. What I think simply doesn't matter anymore. What you think matters. A fresh, young, *individual* perspective is what's really best for this company and for the world. Don't you agree?"

She nodded, brow still knitted.

It was, I admit, gratifying to make such use of my unsung facility for justifying my own inertia. I was born to concoct arguments like this.

"I can't tell you how much this means to me. The fact is, everything else aside, I simply can't bear it. I was hoping to go *shopping*."

"I'm sorry about Wade," she managed. "It must be hard."

"One more thing," I said, inspired. Another avenue for the poor thing. I could almost hear my father's emu celebrating my psychological penetration. "It might be better if I have some public presence now. Kindly begin handling my social media stuff. Don't spend too much time. Just whatever you like. I assure you I won't be looking."

This, at least, was truth.

"You're going to have a lot of followers if you're at all active," she cautioned. "I'm pretty sure people like you have whole PR teams for their social."

I laughed, as if finding this as absurd as it was. Wade, of course, had had a PR team. "Until I can make such arrangements," I said, "I would be grateful if you got things started. I simply don't have the *bandwidth*."

I remained unfit to tease from her look whether she was taking all this as a viable temporary alternative or humoring me.

"Come," I said. "The stuff's in my office."

It felt very businesslike handing reports over to one's intern, and for some time after she left I sat upright at my desk, almost tranquil—maybe in the last hours I'd exhausted my store of anxious neurotransmitters. Maybe I really didn't eat enough. I seemed anyway for the moment back outside my old balloon of care. Vegetatively I gazed at the aloe plant I had never myself watered, imagining that I was clambering up the huge green slopes and sledding down, and sometimes, where opportunity presented, jumping from one to another, revolving slowly in air. I turned with envy to the tiny, bioluminescent sea creatures of my paperweight. It may be after all that our difficulty, our awkward and petulant occupation of the natural world, is merely an accident of our enormous size, and had we remained down among the rodents, lice, paramecia and so on that comprise the lower ninety-nine percent of animal life, we might have retained a sense of proportion and humility. And yet we had been more or less natural once, the natives and so on. Perhaps we were just going through puberty, the great, confused, raging adolescents of earth. Perhaps we would yet come out the other side. The eddy chip implants, which I would no longer be able to suppress, might be equipped with some perceptual amplifications, making of one's desk a *desk*, one's life *life*. I swiveled to the window. The ashen arc of earth spread below the twilight gradient, russet shading away through yellow and dewy white like a strip of skin above stockings. A draft of desire ruffled me.

CHAPTER SIXTEEN

I PUT IN A final standoff with the cursor, a last tug at my own fiber before the summit talk. A horrible thought interrupted me: I would have to give the summit talk.

I had apparently until now not quite believed in its reality, except in the remote abstract, had even disbelieved, all the while secretly, ignominiously suspecting that in the end, having told myself I'd tried, I would hand it off to Palmer and wash my hands of my life. Handing it off to Palmer was now out of the question. But that Zoraida would come up with something I could just edit a bit and sound the Sky-Yacht-worthy visionary in the eyes of the board and the world seemed suddenly shaky, a fantasy of desperation.

The right thing to do remained to skip the summit, direct Goldfarb to make for the aurora borealis before it was too late. Zoraida wouldn't like it, but there was still my potential as a social media figure. Pass over the plutocrats, straight to the people. Anyway, maybe in the meanwhile she would be identified and arrested. How to avert that, avert the summit, avert the future altogether?

Deep as I was in thought, it could no longer be pretended that Palmer hadn't taken up opposite at my desk in a particularly fluorescent state of self-mastery. The planes of his cheeks were flushed, the lovely green eyes flashing.

Persuaded I had registered him, he said, "Can I assume you haven't seen this?" Whatever it was on his eddy.

I extended a palm.

There I was. Surrounded by glinting blue, I floated face-up, sunglassed, slack, swimsuit a faded pink. The photo led an article headlined "Eddy Chief Floats Along" in the Times business section. Stoutmeier wasn't credited, but it was clear enough. The caption quoted me, "Why shouldn't we have shanty towns in Ohio or whatever that is? Why should we always be above everyone?" Beneath this was footage of last night's exercises at the pool, colorful, cheery, ending in a closeup of Palmer himself struggling in the cloud intern's headlock. She looked triumphantly murderous, while Palmer appeared to be in the last stages of suppressing a smile more genuine than I knew he had in him.

> With this year's closely watched Emergent Policy Summit looming, and eddy still playing its hand close, the atmosphere aboard the famous floating headquarters suggests less the final throes of the human era than those of an elite summer camp. Personifying this out-of-step decadence is the reclusive Chris Curtis, Interim Chief Officer since the death of Wade Aubrey last Wednesday. From his private pool atop the grand...

The author at length deigned to introduce me as the co-inventor of emu technology and the originator of the aerial corporate office before bringing me up to the present with a sentence on my questionable connection to eddy's business, research, or other activities of the last two decades. The rest was a speculation on my longstanding manipulation of the perhaps emotionally unsophisticated late savant, my rumored mental derangement from a faulty chip implant, a rundown of my daily floating regimen, affection for flashy clothes, expensive sunglasses, back-to-nature mysticism, and, most unfairly, fine dining. It was rather frivolous reporting.

Palmer hadn't sat. The poor fellow extended a palm, and I placed the eddy in it.

"You have to sue him," he said, "and the Times, and write a letter to the editor, right now. I'll take care of wringing his fat fucking neck. And I'm personally overseeing the change of personnel next time, if there is a next time. This is basic."

"Why would he do this?"

Palmer seized my paperweight, with the living, bioluminescent world. "Because he's *making money* to do this. Because he tricked you and whatever idiot let him up here, I'm guessing Jake. Because this is the big scoop right now, and tomorrow the scoop will be the summit mayhem and his exclusive access up here won't mean top dollar anymore. And *maybe*," Palmer permitted himself a glare, "because that was all you gave him."

"He seemed a decent fellow, in his way," I said weakly.

I was hurt. I had set aside my own romantic futilities to be this man's fairy godmother. I was deeply, unexpectedly wounded.

"He's cashing in at *your* expense," insisted Palmer. "Doesn't that bother you?"

"What can I do? It's more or less accurate. I don't think we have a case."

Palmer lay the paperweight down, thankfully without violence.

"Chris, I was in the room when you came up with eddy. Not emus and all that, I mean the name *eddy*. I know you're not actually brain-damaged. Can't you pull it together for just this week? Maybe you can't sue, but write a letter to the Times. Do something. You're about to give our talk. This is your company too."

"I know. I'm sorry."

"I'm sorry."

Palmer removed himself.

I returned to the ever so slightly curved window. Sparse early stars shone through my dilute reflection. Stoutmeier must have needed money badly, the wretch. It couldn't have been comfortable for him to publish this while still aboard. What especially troubled me was that now Zoraida wouldn't have the consolation of speaking through a credible figure. I pulled up the story and read it over, my life laid in a narrow column.

To the editor, I began, and switched to a call.

"Hey, old CR," said my father's voice, age-scored, smiling. CR stood for Christopher Robin. He'd called me that. Everyone had. People who didn't even know my name was Christopher still somehow instinctively did it. "What's new?" asked the voice, tickled as ever that it was me on the line.

"I'm going to tell you what's new. Ready? The Sky Yacht is almost surely on its last flight. I don't know anyone who even knew us anymore, I mean the family. I shudder to think what I'm going to do with my life, which I notice is more than half over. I spent it pretending to like my only real friend because he could get me out of an ordinary, stupid existence, and I wound up with an even stupider one, which I suppose I deserve. The whole world has become a hateful semi-wasteland, which I will shortly have to return to. And you're—" I couldn't tell him. "You're all I've got," I said instead.

There was a pause as the emu computed all this, just as my father would have paused before saying, "*Oh bud.* I'm sorry."

But the emu didn't speak. Nearly a minute passed.

I checked that the call was still going. It was.

I heard a sob.

"Dad?"

"I'm sorry," the voice wheezed. A pitiful wheeze. I had never heard my father do anything like it. I hung up immediately and called back. He didn't answer. He had never not answered. I didn't know it was a possibility. For a moment the thought flared through me that all this time I had accidentally been talking to my real father, who had, through medical advances escaping my attention, mustered some lucidity. And I had managed to say things I wanted to say, to be with him who I wanted to be, and was. My phone rang. It was him.

"I'm sorry," he said. "You surprised me. I thought you were all right up there."

"I didn't know you could call me."

"I'm not supposed to."

"Dad! I'll come visit. I will. I couldn't stand it. I couldn't stand to see you like that. I don't know how other people do it. How quickly they assimilate the unthinkable. Maybe I'm missing a piece. Remember when I had to be taken out of class when we read Peter Rabbit?"

"Oh yes," he said, recalling. "You wanted a rabbit, didn't you?"

"No. They *kill* his father!"

He was an emu. Blushing in the empty office, I cursed my eager heart.

"I'm sorry I wasn't more open," I said.

"You didn't want to worry me," he said. "You can worry me."

"I know," I said. "I have to go."

"Let me tell you something first."

"Yes?"

"You don't know how good you are."

"I know. I know."

"Listen, you arrogant prick, listen to your father for a second. You think you're soft. You don't know how soft. I could hardly even play a game with you. I would be trying to let you win. You would be trying to let me win. And sticking with Wade all through seventh, eighth, when you should have had more friends, more like yourself, and you could have, you know, by snapping your fingers. I should have made you. You never seemed to suffer like Wade. You had more imagination. You had a wonderful imagination. You think you took advantage, but I wonder where Wade would be without you."

"Probably the same place he is now, and I doubt the others here will take quite as warm an interest in my imaginings," I said with ungrateful irritation. Surely my motives toward Wade were never so pure as my father's emu supposed. Even when I was a boy it must have been really some variant of cowardice, if maybe an imaginative one. "Dad, I just somehow let it slip by me. Just a few modifications, a few adjustments here and there, and I could have actually lived."

"That's what everyone thinks at some point if they're honest with themself."

"Is that what you think? At least you had mom."

"You have people. You can't be someone like you and not have people who love you. I do, you know, and I'm not easy," said the emu. "How about that?"

"You should write this letter to the Times for me. I better get to that. One thing?"

"Yes?"

"What did you mean you're not supposed to call me?"

"It's not part of the defined behaviors."

"You know? You've known?"

"I figured it out. That's what made me so sad for you. No offense."

"You haven't been all that open with me, either, have you?"

There was a lifelike, uncomfortable pause.

"Will you still call me?" said the voice finally.

"Of course."

"You're really all I have. Literally."

"I have to go," I said, although not ahead of a quaver. I couldn't isolate what it was exactly, but it was too much. I hung up, crawled into the hanging acrylic orb chair, and swung myself to sleep.

CHAPTER SEVENTEEN

A THROB, WHICH IN my outgoing dream had been the pulse of a womblike world it was my task to translate before it vanished forever, buzzed in the acrylic against my head.

"Dilworth?" My voice sounded strange in the dark office. No reply.

I oozed down from the orb, out into the hall. The throbbing was here too. The savant hive was abandoned. It must have been late. I followed the disturbance to the main pool.

The chlorine and chaos of a childhood pool party swirled with the rum fumes of frat parties I'd worked at the beginning of all this, before anyone knew me, to produce a startled, reflexive happiness. As on the night before, a mass of colorfully swim-capped interns watched some doings in the water. Once more, on the high lifeguard seat teetered Jake, grand belly slick with perspiration. Closer by were the fully clothed backs of Palmer and our chief counsel Hollingsworth, who must also have come to see about the racket.

"Team building," I said, behind them.

They half-turned their slick heads on me, curious, respectful, unwelcoming.

"Team building," I repeated.

Surely they'd heard of it, of the wild charades imposed in

its name by the most serious people in cufflinks for the most serious ends. It seemed to be working. Never had I seen the interns so enthusiastically engaged. What did it matter that old Jake wasn't pretending at fun for the sake of corporate devotion, but pretending at corporate devotion for the sake of fun? It was a special pity to thwart such a man. He must have decided for himself that I didn't stand a chance of keeping the Sky Yacht going after this flight, and was just trying to get what he could out of the final months. One couldn't blame him. He would never have anything like this in life again. None of us would.

Palmer and Hollingsworth returned to each other with a look not devoid of twinkle. Something was being clinched. I sprang around them toward my old friend on the lifeguard chair, giving a firm cut-throat desist gesture.

He lowered beaming, insane eyes on me.

"Chris! Mr. Curtis hasn't been hit! Have you? We have one more eligible contestant!"

"No, no, Jake. Not now. In fact, it's my regrettable duty—"

"I don't have to remind you, ladies and gentlemen, what's at stake here!" he boomed over me. A pause, as he prepared to remind us what was at stake, and I might have got in a word, but someone was trying to fit a clammy piece of rubber over my head and this was all the moment could hold. It was my friend from the sweat lodge ceremony, the woman who had tricked me into downing a third cup of the potion. Her deeply processed hair was wild—evidently it was her own cap on offer. She looked to be in or near a blackout. Nodding wide-eyed encouragement, having now overcome the obstacle of my ears, she led me by the arm around to the near corner of the pool, the blue corner. The interns we passed fell quiet.

I was sorry to have this effect. The note of high frivolity faded. Cheering stopped.

"Please," I said. "This is all very admirable in terms of participation, but—"

"This is my friend," Jake's amplified voice informed the crowd, filling with sudden sentiment. "My good friend. Even if he is a Cloud-Scraping bastard!" Dutifully, uncertainly, my blue-capped fellows booed. "I know this man! Not only is he our esteemed interim chief, but an interim chief of tremendous vision. Would your average company honcho have any part of this? We're all together here. We all, all of us"—he made a wide, butter-churning gesture—"belong. But I ask you, does it look like this man has a drink? What kind of interns are you?"

A more sincere, general booing at this.

"Now, now," Jake broke in. "The Cloud Scrapers, or whatever you blue people are, defeated piteously in combat here tonight, have one last chance to pull off a miracle. Chris, do you have a swimsuit? Who am I asking? I recognize those bottoms from the Times. Enter the ring, my old friend."

A hand fell on my shoulder. Another reached out to high five. Excited, intoxicated eyes under the blue caps met mine with kinship and frivolous hope.

Those eyes and hands.

"You got this," said someone.

I looked around for Zoraida but couldn't pick her out. *This*, however, I observed, standing on an alligator-shaped float in the middle of the pool beside an untenanted float of the same sort, holding a padded jousting pole, was a strapping young woman in mauve cap, plainly a college athlete. We exchanged an uncertain glance. Jake should have seen that this was not a comfortable situation for either of us.

"I concede defeat," I said. "Give this young person who would have beaten me whatever honors she might deserve, and now if you don't mind—"

"What?" He genuinely hadn't heard.

But my blue friends looked at me as if betrayed, and I found myself having uttered, "Stoutmeier. I'll take Stoutmeier."

I sent a meaning glance to Palmer. Among all those bodies the young COO looked not so out of place, and even Hollingsworth, with his sleek grey hair, bullfrog neck, and moist, downturned lips, looked appropriately amphibious. I was sure Stoutmeier would have no part of it, even on the chance he wasn't hiding out in his berth.

"Stoutmeier? Oh Bob!" Jake, at least, was delighted at this turn. "I don't believe he's been hit either. Bob Stoutmeier!" he yelled, and that would have ended it, and I would have shut the thing down, definitely, had Stoutmeier, like the very devil, not materialized beside the bar, on which he laid his big, professional camera. He took a peevish, quizzical pace forward.

"Do you need a swimsuit?" asked Jake.

Stoutmeier waved this off and, to my surprise—and surprising, sudden physical fright—called for the float to be pushed right up to the edge. The mauve champion dismounted her plastic alligator and swam it over as the journalist removed his boat shoes.

At last, standing precariously on the oblong floats, ringed in by round-headed, earless, pretty creatures, the two dusty, middle-aged men, neglected writer and vapid subject, faced one another. Our weapons were plastic poles with foam pads like marshmallows on either end. Jake started up some deafening exordium, and my grotesque double was upon me. The blow was glancing, and the next I dodged. I was, at least, a slight target. Ingeniously using my marshmallow as a paddle while Stoutmeier caught his balance, I moved in.

I imagine exorcists feel this way, in the beginning.

Such raw release I had never experienced. I grew formidable with it, towering. I fell on the wretch with an almighty whirlwind.

"Ingrate! Sellout! Self-hater! Lazy, thoughtless, *dowdy*—"

Surfacing, wiping my hair aside, I found Stoutmeier calling for one of his team to tow him back in. Amid uncertain congratulations, he retrieved his camera.

I saw myself through its eye: a drenched rat in a designer shirt being pulled from the water by half-naked, drunken women half his age. I looked for Palmer, but he and Hollingsworth were gone. Someone tossed me a towel.

CHAPTER EIGHTEEN

> The level of mass self-deception is just exquisite. I keep head-shouting back at these reports. I guess I'm writing that speech. I really can't stop.

The call that supplanted this brief entry was to an emu, not of her father but herself, with an input boundary of one year previous—herself, that is, of the year before. I opted for playback.

"Hey," said the high, strong voice, "it's me, you of next year. Sorry to break it to you that you're not a real person, but we don't have time to be delicate."

"Yeah yeah. Who is this?" demanded the high, strong voice.

"It's you, and we have to get up in two hours. Zoraida, you're an emu. Just face it and listen. You're supposed to be the hardcore one anyway."

"I knew it," snapped former Zoraida. "We're going soft."

"Please just listen."

"Are you on the Sky Yacht?"

"Yes, but—"

"*But?*" The emu interrupted. "Did we not anticipate that things might feel different when the time came? Did we not promise ourself to ignore the suddenly *extenuating* circumstances?"

"Things got weird. Wade is already dead, and I just found out there's a gas leak. There could be casualties."

A pause. At last former Zoraida said, "Obviously this is easier for me to say, but that's why you called. I think we don't abandon the larger picture for the sake of a few tech bros."

"They're not even tech bros."

"Whatever. I'm sorry, but do you think Abraham Lincoln said, 'I just found out that my Union army is made up of individual human beings, call the whole thing off. Sorry, slaves.'?"

"I've read everything you've read about Lincoln. Maybe take it down a notch and try to empathize for a second."

"*Take it down a notch?* Do I become an old lady in one year?"

Zoraida sighed. "I'm just going to delete you and start again."

"No, sorry. Go on," the emu said with genuine, spooked urgency, making herself agreeable.

"Okay, so the other factor is that Chris Curtis is basically vegetative. I think he has some issues from one of those chip implants, which is why eddy stopped making them. I get the impression he's on his way out now that Wade Aubrey's gone, and he's tasked me to write his summit talk and take over his social. He seems to genuinely give not a fuck. I kind of really want to do this. Tell me it's pointless."

"It's pointless."

"Is it? We're talking about a white mega-wealthy male, and as far as anyone knows one of the big tech gods. This is the kind of person people actually listen to. This is someone with real leverage. And he's mine."

"Oh, now you finally get to be a rich white guy and everything's changed? Do you hear what you're saying? I might just hang up and delete myself."

"You think I'm delusional?"

"*Yes.* You got yourself—or I got you—onto the Sky Yacht. I can't believe this gas leak is going to be the sticking point. I'm going to figure this out for you. Tell me more."

"One gas bladder is leaking, which means that if I set off the charges, and it's one of the other bladders that's leaking, we don't have time to evacuate."

"How do you ignite the charges?"

"Fabio made an app. I just tap a button, it sends a signal to the detonators I stuck on the squeegee bots."

"And you have how many bots in place?"

"One for each of the five bladders, but the timing is sequential. The first three go right away, then there's a delay while we evacuate. It should still be pretty high up when the whole thing blows."

"And you can't adjust the ignition sequence?"

"I'm not senile. It's not like that didn't occur to me."

"Did it occur to you to ask Fabio to send a new version of the app where only two of the charges go off right away?"

"No. No, actually. You're a genius."

"Thank you. Now do I need to stay on here with you for the rest of our life? I will, if that's what I have to do."

"God, I really have gotten stupider. This is worrying."

"That or you didn't want to find the solution."

"It wasn't conscious, Z."

"I know it wasn't conscious," the emu conceded.

"But still I'm going to write the speech, and I want to make Mr. Curtis say things on social. People will listen to him who will just never listen to us, whatever we do."

"What is this, Zoraida? Have we been talking? Are you sure you're not the emu?"

"I mean I might as well wait till after the talk. It's not the very last thing at the summit. Why not do both?"

"Hmmm."

"What?"

"You promise, both?"

"Yes. I promise."

The former Zoraida took a deep breath, and, lapsing into a more relaxed tone, asked, "So what else is going on?"

"Nothing much. Tired. Lonely as hell. We almost banged Morgan Palmer."

The emu burst into raucous, snorting laughter.

I stopped listening.

"Dilworth?"

"Yeah?" He didn't sound sleepy.

"Please give the cloud intern the morning off. And send me the physical security person when he's up."

"Is everything all right?" he asked, excited.

"Yes, it's nothing to worry about, Dilworth. Tell them not to bring breakfast."

I would have to turn Zoraida in first thing after sunrise, and I didn't see how I could watch it beside her.

CHAPTER NINETEEN

THE SUN COMPRESSED ITSELF on the horizon, oblong, as if reconsidering. Clouds were few. I looked down. A river had overflown its banks, tracing out in reflected rose the grid of a city, buildings still hardly discernible in haze. I strained to see if boats were cruising the submerged streets. When I was a boy and flooding on this scale was still an eminently newsworthy phenomenon, I felt the deepest envy for the people pictured floating in canoes past second-floor windows. The headmistress glided around the port-side curve.

"Chris," said a low voice.

I turned to find not the security man but a strangely subdued Morgan Palmer.

"Ah, Palmer," I said, putting a hand to my chest. "Will you get yourself some tap shoes, for pity's sake?"

He gave a toned-down version of the look that indicated I was once again not apprised of something. "I sent you a message. Last night," he said.

"I'm sorry, I didn't see."

Rattled by Palmer's tone, I checked my eddy. I had a number of new messages, items on which I had been cc'ed, which I ignored as a rule, and one from Palmer asking whether I had read in particular the one regarding restructuring. I scanned for it, pulse sounding in my ears. Vaguely I wondered if the subject line would read *restructuring* or, absurdly, *re: restructuring*. It was the former. I slid down to the deck, resting my back against the rail.

What we dread we nevertheless imagine coming on gradually, humanely. We do ourselves that kindness, however often in reality events leave us like someone a second to the wrong side of the guillotine. After an emergency session late last night, the board was agreed that in view of the escalating frequency of credible threats, as well as the collapse of the professional working environment and associated concerns for safety, publicity, and potential legal action, the Sky Yacht was no longer tenable as eddy corporate headquarters. Following the summit the executive team would relocate to the Florham Park facility. I laid my forehead on the bridge of my folded arms.

"I'm sorry," came Palmer's attempted sympathy above.

"I suppose I can't be surprised," I said.

I had been so absorbed in my talk, my chances, in tantalizing portents and anxieties, I had neglected the obvious, the ordinary. I should have kept a firmer hold on Jake, Stoutmeier, everything. I should have been an interim chief.

"I know how you feel about this place," Palmer commiserated, "but it would be extremely destructive to go to war with the board now."

"I can't really detain you all here, can I?"

"No."

"Well?" I said, looking up with a hostility that surprised us both.

"You understand this means we'll no longer be supporting the Sky Yacht as a corporate property."

"I understand."

"We'll find something in the city next quarter. Nice and high-up. Good views." He did feel sorry for me.

"So we'll be landing after the conference?"

"We might as well make it before."

"I wouldn't advise that," I said. It wasn't entirely reflex. "Given our threat status, I mean, it might not be advisable to make a sudden, unexpected move. The person in question might see their chance vanishing and accelerate things."

Palmer of course took this as mere flailing to avoid the ground.

"If I believed in this *threat*, I would think landing sooner than later would be a good thing. You, Hollingsworth, and I can stay aboard till the conference is over. The others can start heading to Florham Park, get things set up. We can leave the yacht where we land until we figure out how to dispose of it."

Dispose of it. Audibly, humiliatingly, I gasped.

Palmer absorbed himself in his timepiece.

"I have to caution us not to land," I reiterated. "I am interim chief."

"Don't do this, Chris. It's no use. I really am sorry how things have turned out. I realize you're not having an easy month." He touched my shoulder, about level with his hand. Then, more gently, "It'll be all right. Give it a chance. It could be a good change."

I returned my head to the bridge of my arms. The next time I saw my sky, it would be pressed up against a paper-sized airplane window.

CHAPTER TWENTY

I FLOATED, RANGING OVER the course of my life, from start to various endings. *Are we having such a good time here?* I heard in repeating voiceover, and that bit about the exchange value of the indefinite something or other of one tepid life.

One tepid life.

At some point Jake appeared to discuss another gala event. Executive hadn't told him this would be our last night aloft, or they had and this was his finale. I didn't really listen. Once he was gone, whether from prolonged stress or having eaten nothing since yesterday's smoothie, I drifted gratefully from consciousness.

I woke in twilight. A magma-red hourglass loomed over the world. It was a moment before I could identify it as the just-risen, atmospherically magnified moon, partly obscured by sky-colored clouds. We were already making our descent. I had missed the last sunset. Throwing on the velour pants and slippers, I rushed down the spiral stairs to the observation deck. A figure stood at the westward rail. I had neglected to give her the evening off. I had neglected to turn her in. Maybe it was no longer unavoidable. The fact was I couldn't bear that decision on top of everything else. I had hardly thought of it.

"Where were you?" she said. "It was a good one. Are you okay?"

"You watched the whole thing?"

"I've been here."

That was some strange relief.

"Thank you," I said.

We stood in our accustomed silence, though there seemed an appeal or prompt in her eyes.

"I'm sorry for how things have turned out," I said uncertainly.

The eyes were unsure what I meant. So Executive still hadn't made it public. She hadn't even heard from Palmer.

"The Sky Yacht is being discontinued," I said shortly, voice steady. I wasn't sure how she'd take this, whether to tell her we'd be landing before the summit.

She took it harder than I'd imagined. She looked nonplussed, then, oddly, saddened, then less saddened.

"*Good*," she said finally. "I'm sorry to be the one to tell you this, but the Sky Yacht was kind of a major middle finger to the rest of us."

"People love the Sky Yacht."

"I know." Again she looked pained, perhaps remembering her own long-ago Sky Yacht selfie. "I was going to address that in your speech."

My speech.

"You haven't read the Times lately, have you?"

"I saw the piece," she said.

"I'm sorry. Not what we wanted, I suppose."

"Mr. Curtis, have you seen your follower numbers? For someone whose company owns major stakes in the socials, you don't seem to have much grasp on what the public wants to see."

"That I wouldn't dream of denying, but I don't know how anyone who read that so-called article could see me as anything other than a vapid, reckless, narcissistic semi-imbecile."

"I know. It's almost as though they're trying to position you for a presidential run. Your following was up over thirty million as of my last post. Wait." She checked. "Eighty-one."

I put my head in my hands.

"Do you want to talk about the speech now?" she said, pleased.

"No."

"Mr. Curtis, I'm sorry about your *yacht*, but don't tell me you're backing out."

"What difference does it make? Do you think anything I could say would change anything? You don't really think that. You've just convinced yourself to think that for the moment."

She looked as though I'd slapped her.

"I have that contract," she said.

"It won't work."

"Hey, I never thought the summit would make any difference either, but it *could*. I started writing something, and I want you to look at it."

"I'm sure it's good, but—"

"But? What are you going to say down there?"

"I'm not going to say anything. Benevolent corporate dictatorship, cloud mirrors, some other desperation. I won't be a part of it. And I'm not going down there. I'm not leaving the Sky Yacht." I heard the petulance in my voice, but it was truth. I wasn't leaving. I saw that now. I would chain myself to something if necessary. I seized the rail with both hands. Zoraida watched, appalled.

"You're a child," she said, more in wondering observation

than censure. "Sorry. I guess I don't care all that much about my eddy internship. Can you imagine that?"

"No!" I said, not in response, but in general protest. I couldn't just then think how to elaborate.

She could. There was no use patronizing me anymore. She let out, "You're not even a child. You're an infant. It's no wonder you don't eat solid food."

Something, I couldn't tell whether rage, shame, some combination, something else entirely, stood my hairs on end.

"I thought you would understand," I said, "that words won't . . . Action . . . *Action.* Don't you agree?"

She hiked her shoulders, put up her palms. What was I telling her, Zoraida?

"I mean we have to *act*. Words don't work anymore. Images don't work anymore. Right? That's what I'm going to say."

"We have to act by not abandoning our yacht?"

"Yes! You have to make a stand, do what you believe. You've inspired me. You gave me an idea."

It was an idea, after all, that had set my hairs on end. I knew what I had to do.

"Jake is gathering everyone at the pool again," I said. "I'll give my talk there. My own talk. It may have already begun. Come."

Moody red light glided over the big pool, arteries pouring into lazy red organs, splitting, draining. For now the interns were dressed, and nicely. With a pang, I imagined them only a week ago packing with anticipation this or that attractive after-work item. What might await them! It was already hard to remember what anyone ever did at night before Jake's disastrous reign. Probably worked. Even so, the folk had yet to attain the pitch of hilarity in which I had lately found them. It was early. A line trailed from the makeshift bar. Young people stood or sat among the beach chairs, faces aglow in the light of eddies, darkening to talk to those present or look around for someone. There was muted laughter, a springy quiet of incipient fun, and I hoped here and there one of them was secretly leading a tour for the older person they might become—*Here you were, on the Sky Yacht, now hardly more than a dream we had—Oh, this fellow, remember him? How he pretended not to adore us, how goofy he was. And here is Kelly, who just visited the house along with her new dreadful husband—Imagine you and she still hardly liked each other then!* Perhaps the photos they snapped, intended, of course, to publicize rather than preserve, would serve them in time.

Some actual older women, presumably meditation students, were present. They knew, as the interns didn't, that this would be their last night above the clouds. The executive team was elsewhere, I suppose in eager conclaves over the new regime. A dj rig had been set up alongside the bar, where now a girl who looked no more like a dj than she did an egret, with great concentration was wiring in an additional gadget, ignoring shouted requests from those waiting for punch. The music was actually pleasant: flying-saucery and low.

I was against the wall by the shallow end, lounging nearly full length, there being no real alternative, on a padded white beach chair. Maybe this illusory relaxed posture was responsible for the approach of the odd intern cluster, wanting to take a picture with me. Perhaps these people were my followers. I spotted Zoraida by the door, in the company of Stoutmeier. They watched me submit to a small group photo, after which

I watched myself, as though from a height, make my way to the lifeguard station and mount the steps to the platform, on which I quickly realized I could not stand. I felt excessively long and thin, like a hot dog, all those pretty, innocent faces turning on me like the mirrors of a reflector oven, cooking me. I longed for a bun, some insulation. So many fine, open faces. All this time, all of these flights, I really never got to know any of them. I sat on the high chair. The room quieted.

Behind the bar, Jake flapped a hand at the egret dj, who stopped the music. He came around, got hold of the mic, and grandly approached, reaching it up to me like Lady Liberty. All at once the idea that had thrilled my every follicle up on deck seemed foolish, delusive, and in need of considerable if not infinite introductory hemming.

"Ladies and scant gentlemen," I said, overloud into the mic. I pulled it back and proceeded inaudibly, "What do we do all day?"

No response came.

"One thing it seems to me we don't do enough of is look around." The person at whom I was staring, and perhaps had been staring at for some time, was the headmistress. I had never before seen her at the pool. "On the other hand," I amended, "I suppose your own internal environment may be very rich and even a pleasure to anyone fortunate enough to find themself in those parts. In fact, I hope you at times welcome such travelers, especially your elders." I had in mind the tours, of the sort that had just occupied my reveries, which I hoped the young people were giving their older selves. From the headmistress's expression, and that of her neighbors, however, it seemed this endorsement of elders traveling into them was being taken in another way. Here and there, first one, then another, then everywhere, emerged eddies. The moment was being recorded, or broadcast, to be rebroadcasted indefinitely. Through a hundred sleek little holes in space and time, the world peered in. Had I never dreamed this? Is there a person alive who never once raved in his heart to all humanity? Faces looked now predominantly not at me, but at the smaller me in the hands. Maybe they were all just getting the light and sound up to the standards their followers had a right to expect. Anyway, it was somewhat relieving not to be the center of attention. By the door, Zoraida too held up her eddy. Stoutmeier shot with his professional camera.

"My dear people," I said more ingratiatingly, "I'm sorry we aren't better acquainted. You wouldn't guess how much I like to see you around the place."

I had not found the note, the faces said. I continued, "I love especially to see you in the dining hall getting to know each other, becoming friends. That's all over, as of today." I seemed to be giving a graduation speech. "You'll never again be thrown together with people so like yourselves, eating and living under the same dome. Well, I hope some of you will have a family—maybe with someone you met here—but you won't meet people again like you did on the Sky Yacht, or at school, or at camp. There's simply no mechanism for it in adult life. My dear children, you'll just about die of loneliness. Think of it. You'll work all day in your pjs, or commute with silent, exhausted people by the hundreds packed all around, on the train, in cars. You'll never know them. You'll eat at your desk. You'll sing karaoke with your officemates because HR will make you. You'll convince yourself you like a couple of them. You'll talk about shows. My god, will you talk about shows. You'll talk about sports. Huge amounts of alcohol will be needed. And then I hope you'll remember it here. You'll remember . . ."

I was looking down at Jake, whom I could remember from so ludicrously long ago. He looked back blankly.

"I go to the dining hall," I resumed, "just to see you splendid people together. It's the highlight of my day. As to what you intend to do with the rest of your life, it grieves me to think. Your *life*." I made a fist. I meant it. "What do you plan to do after this?"

Again no reply.

"What's really waiting for you down there? It's not at all your kind of place, down there, just savage on every level. It's no longer hospitable to the sensitive, intelligent likes of yourselves. What will you most fortunate people do in this grievous time? You'll get the jobs you're after. You'll look at a glowing device. Your life will go into it. It's going into it *right now*. Look up. My dear people, *look up!*"

A few dear people actually did look up, then down again. Zoraida looked up.

"Now I have to make an awful announcement. The Sky Yacht is being grounded, as of later tonight. We won't fly again. You won't see each other again. I won't see you again. Your life as adults lamentably commences."

Gasps did not ring out, but there was a change in the quality of attention. The news of their internships being canceled was not trivial. I wondered if their internships really were canceled. Maybe there was some arrangement for them in Florham Park. Maybe their parents would get them apartments nearby.

"Tomorrow," I continued, "you go into the world. You imagine awaiting you not the world, but the *world*. I hope anyway you don't just imagine that you're going to start work at eddy or wherever it is for the next fifty-odd years, if there are fifty-odd more years. Well, I don't feel good releasing you into this so-called world. Who in her right mind would want to leave this place for that one?"

At this point, although I by no means thought myself a fan favorite, I was surprised to be not only answered, but heckled. It was Zoraida. From back by the door came the high voice, "Someone who doesn't just worry about *his* own ass!"

"Exactly," I said. "My cloud intern, everyone. Maybe we should lose the eddies for this next bit. It's important we control the story from here on somewhat more deliberately. Stoutmeier will be a great help in that area, won't you, Bob? Now, in your pockets, please. I'll resume when I see everyone's empty hands in the air."

Curiosity, I imagine more than obedience, prevailed, and eddies gradually sank. At last the room faced me, uneasily, hands in air, as in the crucial first moments of a bank heist.

"I've decided I'm not going down. I'm staying put. The cooks may go, the food will run out, I will be up here until the world becomes hospitable. I invite you all to join me. From this moment, as a matter of fact, I will eat nothing further. Nothing solid, anyway."

Again Zoraida's high voice pierced the room, "You already don't eat!"

"Please join me. Any changes you want to see, I mean, any protests against anything you may want to publicize, just tell Zoraida there and she'll add it to her list. You can leave anytime of course. There will be helicopters for whoever wants to go."

It struck me that without my having noticed it, in the

stealthy way of clouds, the audience had shifted its center of mass. It had moved away from me, toward the exits.

"Now I'm not saying it will be easy," I said, holding up a hand. "One inconvenience I might as well mention up-front. We'll be hunger striking on a famous airborne luxury yacht above a pivotal international summit with press from all over the world. We'll naturally be a somewhat heavily played news item. If you stay your names and likenesses may be used. You may be called upon to appear on camera, to talk to our journalist, you may of course be posting about it yourself. Your followings may balloon a bit overwhelmingly. People may recognize you on the streets afterward. I'm sorry, but that's the nature of the thing."

With great stealth, again, the interns now seemed to have moved a step closer, back toward me.

"We wouldn't really starve, right?" said someone, a familiar voice. I located the boy—Dilworth?—standing close beneath.

"No, at least not right away. We have some amount of smoothie supplies. Very nutritious stuff. You may get thinner. You may at least want to look a little thinner after a few days for the cameras. That is, let's not mention the smoothies publicly. I suppose you may know something about your thin angles on camera?"

A few heads nodded.

Possible-Dilworth said, "And we don't have to do anything but post and do interviews and hang out?"

"You're *prohibited* from doing anything else."

"What about drinks?" Jake asked. "Is that food?"

"No, I don't suppose so."

He started noisily lining up a bar-length row of shots.

"I'm not sure that's quite in the spirit, Jake."

"What about bar snacks? You have to eat a little something if you're going to drink."

"Fine, limited bar snacks," I conceded.

"I've got twenty-five hundred pickled eggs," he said. "I thought I wouldn't get to use them."

He gave a signal to the dj and whatever objection I might have raised was lost to a deafening beat and the familiar old lyric . . . *Doing shots with a robot on the motherfucking Sky Yacht.*

The interns converged on the bar.

I made for Zoraida, who stood, arms folded, looking eager for Stoutmeier to emerge from his camera.

"Are you pleased?" I beamed.

"What?"

I recalled I was not really supposed to know her leanings.

"I mean, I hope you don't mind my saddling you with compiling our demands."

The girl steadied herself with a calming, Palmer-esque breath, looking out over the revelers. "As you see," she said, "I'm just inundated."

"Give them time to think. Meanwhile start with your own."

"I'm not participating in this."

"What? Why not?"

"Does this look like a hunger strike? I'm not even your intern anymore. I don't have to indulge your fantasy life."

I didn't know what to say. I could feel myself flattening, giving way under the cloud intern's superior substance. I could tell I looked wounded. Instead of backing off, she attacked with increased gusto.

"What are you actually against? Loneliness? Having to be a grown-up? That's quite a cause. Maybe you should start a foundation for it."

"I'm against what you're against."

"What am I against? Do you know?"

I knew, more or less.

"You don't even *care* what you're against," she shouted over the noise. "As long as you don't have to live on the same planet with the rest of us."

"That isn't fair."

"*Fair?*"

Stoutmeier shot a picture of us.

"Will you stop that, Stoutmeier!" I bellowed.

He put up both of us his hands, as I'd had the others do. He shook them to show he was scared. A number of people looked our way. I wished I were one of them, any of them.

"It's the last night to really see the stars," I muttered, by way of excusing myself, and started up for my own pool.

CHAPTER TWENTY-ONE

AS IT HAPPENED, WE were already under an overcast. Eyes closed, I gently rocked my float, trying to remember the very first Sky Yacht night, a specific shooting star, a specific cloud.

A throat cleared.

"Hello, Palmer."

"We talked about this," came Palmer's voice, forbearing, parental, disappointed.

"I'm not keeping you here."

"You can't really stay."

"Can you stop me? I mean, legally?"

I opened my eyes. Palmer loomed cross-armed on the landing.

"Yes," he said. "It could take a little while, but yes."

"A little while is better than nothing. You go give that talk of yours. I'm sure it will be good. I'll have Goldfarb bring us almost to the ground. You all get off. I won't. That's it."

"What talk of mine?"

"The eddy talk. I hope you don't mind filling in on short notice."

Palmer shunted any elation into his capillaries, straight face reddening to the straight hairline. It was a strangely gratifying sight.

"So I'm giving the eddy talk," he said with composure,

"while you're up here staging a media circus? What I want to do, you know, is not destroy the world. It's also not necessarily unrealistic. You'll be undermining that."

"I know," I said. "Give your talk, get the others behind you. It may not be useless. Meanwhile, I'll be here. We'll see what happens."

"My stock options are going to be worth a roll of stamps is what's going to happen."

"I have faith in you."

Palmer squatted on the landing.

"I guess this is it," he said. "We found some suites in one of the protestor hotels. We won't be back after tonight."

"Will that be pleasant? By all means stay here. You're very welcome."

"We should start distancing ourselves."

"Right."

"But I hope whatever this is passes and we see you in Florham Park. You'll have a space waiting."

"Thank you, Palmer."

We shook hands. I don't know why.

"Bring your intern," he shouted up from the stairs.

Distortions of merriment swelled, echoed in long, flowing braids off the high dome. "Light," I said, and an aquamarine circle appeared faintly above in internal reflection. A rectangular gap in the middle, like a keyhole, was me. I put on my good, clear goggles and rolled off the float, down into the aquamarine depths. I spread my limbs wide to the sky, and watched my breath, in countless wavering cells, escape to the surface.

Playback:
"Hey."

"You again."

"Sorry, were you busy? The Sky Yacht's being decommissioned. Immediately."

"Huh," the emu of former Zoraida absorbed this. "Now or never."

"I thought that for a second too, but a *hunger strike* has been called."

"Against eddy? Good for you guys."

"No, basically by eddy. Chris Curtis anyway. Until the world becomes *hospitable*."

"What the hell does that mean?"

"That's my job to figure out what it means. He just wants to sound like he's not having a tantrum over his yacht. And he wants company."

"And we care because?"

"It could be an opportunity."

"Oh *Zoraida*," moaned the emu. "Listen to your better self. Three completely unambiguous words: Blow. It. Up. Everyone's leaving but the top bastard. You couldn't have planned it better. This is exactly what we wanted when it was Wade Aubrey."

"I know, I know, but Stoutmeier says—"

"Don't quote Stoutmeier to me. I'm not one of those ignoramuses at the Humans office."

"No, he's here. And he says—"

"*What?*"

"I forgot I didn't tell you."

"Bob Stoutmeier is up there and you're fucking Morgan Palmer?"

"I didn't fuck Morgan, and Bob Stoutmeier is a round little old man. He's like sixty now."

"He's Bob Stoutmeier. I'd do it."

"Apparently you wouldn't."

"Pffff."

"Anyway, he claims, and I tend to agree, that hunger strikes are ideally effective, it's just that hardly anyone with influence ever does them, for obvious reasons. Granted, this is a smoothie strike, but the point is we can control the story much better than with a one-off action. It's more sympathetic, more sustained, less susceptible to spin. The situation is pretty perfect. It would be just him, me, and Chris."

"*Chris?*"

"Well, a few others were excited too, for however long that would last. They're sort of pretending to themselves they don't just want to be celebrities. People are actually giving me demands to add to my list."

"What list? This is *ridiculous*."

"You don't think I feel ridiculous? I'm the one getting all spun around every two seconds. I barely sleep. You're just sitting there in a chip or something. Be the rational one and help."

"Okay, let's not make this confusing. Right now the Sky Yacht is still *the* symbol of inequality and mass obliviousness. After your *smoothie strike* it's going to be some weird, ambivalent thing. What does Helen have to say? Does she know?"

"Fuck Helen."

"Fuck *Helen?*"

Helen must have been our H.

"Blasphemy, I know, but I've seen things in the last year and she's really not so different, using people for her own ends like anyone in power. Fabio is clearly just a lost soul they were happy enough to brainwash for his coding skills. He actually wrote me the other day just completely freaked out about everything. I think something weird is going on there."

"Our *ends* are what matters. So not everyone's a saint like you. Could it just be with all this *controlling the story* that you're afraid people in the wrong bubbles aren't going to see what a saint you are? I think you're terrified the world is going to dismiss you and you'll just be rotting away unappreciated, like Berkman. You want to be a star, just like dad said. You'd rather starve to death—make that *pretend* starve to death—than not be a pillar of glory."

"Of course I'm afraid. Of course it's harder when it's tomorrow and not a year away, but I really believe Stoutmeier on this. He's been in a lot more shit than we have. He was at Seattle. He was in *East Timor*."

"Is Stoutmeier going to be starving?"

"No, but he'll cover it."

"See. Here's the problem: whatever you ask for has to happen within a few weeks. After that, the threat dissipates pretty fast."

Zoraida was silent.

"If you know what I mean?" said the emu.

"I don't think the usefulness of it dissipates."

"I admire that. I do. But didn't you say it's fake?"

"Not completely. We really will run out of smoothie stuff at some point."

"Sorry, but I just feel like making farting noises with my mouth right now. You don't think Mr. Sky Yacht might change his mind when his belly starts rumbling?"

"I'm not sure. He has problems. This is not a happy guy. I mean, he's here because he doesn't want to face life. I'm far from convinced he wouldn't rather just get it over. In a way, you can't tell me you don't relate."

"Fine, if neither of you wants to survive, blow yourself up too, but just—"

"Jesus, how do you even know what I'll ask for can't happen in a few weeks?"

"I know because I'm *you*."

"I'm not sure."

"I was you."

"You're so angry, Z," said Zoraida, pained.

"And you're not? What the hell happens to me?"

"What happens to you is you had to write a goodbye to mom, *again*. We wouldn't even be here if reaching the end didn't change the game a little. I think we're entitled. I don't think I'm a saint. I think maybe you're the saint. Maybe I really was. Being a human is another story."

"Playing the human card," observed the emu bitterly. "I know it's not easy, but what were we going to do when we started to feel like this? A mantra helps. Let me suggest a simple three-word example—"

"Why are you so stuck on the Sky Yacht, can you tell me? Tell me."

"I think I have."

"I don't know," Zoraida considered. "I've been having some trouble with this since talking to you. It's a weird, kind of horrifying, sensation, to be honest, like when you see a picture of yourself and everyone says you look normal when you clearly look terrible. I don't know if you get the same effect, as the emu party to this, but somehow I don't feel like I'm talking to myself. I feel like I'm just talking to a friend, or even a stranger, someone I'd want to *help*. I don't think I could tell myself this, but it's almost hilariously obvious listening to you: this is all about you, all that anger, probably it's dad in there, other normal, unsaintly human things. You're using the world's troubles, in a way, a good way, but it's you. And you almost see that. I want to be a pillar of glory, right? You can say that to *me*. You didn't say it to yourself, back then, did you? Right? If I'm doing this, I just have to be sure it's from a real place."

"A *real* place? Jesus Christ. Say what you want about Helen and them, but I swear to you that you were not the fake one in this situation."

"How do you know?"

"You may not know when you're dreaming, but you *know* when you're awake. You're pretending not to. You're the fake now. You're doing a fake hunger strike. Yes, I'm angry. For a reason. You used to know what it was. That reason matters. The personnel, whatever their unconscious motives and all that, I don't care. I don't matter. You don't matter. You're rationalizing. Call me whatever makes you feel better, but you have to see past *yourself* and just—"

"Enough. Enough, Z. I can't stand this anymore. I love you, but I'm erasing you."

CHAPTER TWENTY-TWO

ABOVE SPREAD A THIN parchment, concentrating here and there in long, massy forms like scroll ends. Pink underlining appeared at length, but faint, earthly. I stood awhile after it went, tracking the evolution of the overcast, imagining a conversation with old Chris Curtis of a year before and whether I or anyone could pick out a difference between us.

Through the dome came an irritating buzz. It grew louder and now deafening as the next group made its way into the airlock to board the shuttle helicopters. The exodus had been going steadily for some time.

"Hey."

Zoraida, finally. Her short hair was chaotic with slept-in fixative. She wore the big, prescription glasses I had seen that first night spying.

"I'm sorry for losing it on you last night," she said. "I'm in. I want to talk about what we're going to say."

"That I leave in your hands. I meant what I said."

"I appreciate the confidence, Mr. Curtis, but this is your move. When you're done, it's done, if you know what I mean. I assume we're not staying without you. So we have to talk like people for a minute. First, who exactly are we making this statement to? Who are we making demands of?"

"Who? . . . I suppose everyone."

The neat brows over the big glasses.

"Everyone at the summit," I specified. Surely, the summit.

"Can I show you something?"

"Of course."

She turned her eddy my way.

"No," I said, "thank you."

"Chris. You should understand our situation. Can we watch together for one minute? You can tap out sooner if you feel like you're going to faint. All right? I'm here."

I surrendered.

It was the news. A mirrored cube of conference center glinted under the title *Day 1*. And here the old bizarre, pedantic intonations of newscaster speech, punching blindly every few beats at the first syllable in sight, heedless of meaning, English as whack-o-mole. Heads of state and industry had gathered for the first session of the Emergent Policy Summit. The US interior secretary would lay out the provisions of its ambitious Green Road ahead of the defense minister's case for a joint eco-defense operation with Brazil. Brazil would have its say in the afternoon. Meanwhile, protestors too had gathered.

Happily, things looked more peaceable than they had on my ill-fated James Turrell run of the year before. Between metal cordons, high-spirited citizens chanted to one another and to the impassive visors of riot police in long ranks, quaintly holding curved, clear shields like a medieval general's vision of the future. The camera picked out a group of energetic grey-haired ladies bouncing a banner, *Green Road = Green Load*, to the general chant, "Too little, Too late!" which became, more rhythmically, "Decentralize . . .

Revitalize . . . Smart constitution—end pollution!" which spawned an opposing chant from a similar group under a sign *Smart Constitution = Dumb Solution*: "Cryptocracy . . . Kleptocracy . . . What do we want?"

They wanted democracy. Others chanted, "Accept . . . Adapt . . . Fund survival, not denial!"

"Accept?" I asked. "Adapt?"

"Funny that would pique your interest," said Zoraida. "They want to just accept that we're not going to fix the climate in time, and then use the funding from these expensive Hail Mary's to pay for adaptive strategies, living with the change. There's another group focused on picking up and going to Mars. You might really like them."

"I don't like any of this," I said.

"Okay," she said, putting down the eddy and meeting my eye in checkmate, "What do you like?"

"What do you like?" I parried.

"I like some parts of these positions. I like what I like. Do you want the details? I never meant to impose a particular plan on people. That's pretty much the polar opposite of what I like. I hadn't really thought of making demands."

"Had you thought of something else?"

She looked sharply up, then down. "I want people to want what they want," she said, "but from their own wacky, wounded hearts. I'm not against some system, even a *smart* one, but it has to emerge from what's real, not what we have now. A person is powerful when she can remember to be one, dig out from all this team-building and disgraceful signaling, basically eddying, all this control. Dig out that neglected naked mole rat of a self and take it very, very seriously. Being a weirdo, in other words," she laughed. "That's the only hope I see."

She had looked up at me on *weirdo*, with the self-conscious, laughing gaze, so that I felt she included me, despite herself, despite myself, in that hopeful category.

"Yes, I like that," I said. I was of course already more or less familiar with these ideas from her documents. "Why don't you make your demands from the weirdness of your own stifled heart, and I'll sign on just to save time. After all, we're mainly setting an example, yes?"

She nodded, frowning. "The part I need you to understand," she said, "is that what I'll demand, if I have to get demanding, might not happen so fast. It might not be weeks."

"I won't stop," I said. "I won't leave. I assure you. Never."

"I believe you," she said, uncertainly.

"But?"

"Sorry, but I feel like I'm taking advantage."

"Of?"

She made an abortive gesture toward her head and winced.

"Oh," I said, catching on. "I'm not actually infirm."

"What about the . . . There's a story you have some trouble from trying out that eddy implant that was in the news a while back."

"For goodness sake, I don't have a chip in my head."

This surprised her.

"Then why . . ."

"Yes?"

"Why didn't those implants come out?"

A deft adjustment. I assume the aborted question was nearer *then why would you want to do this, privileged, infinitely lucky you?* Why toss yourself into my hands, into this extremity? Why do this wonderful thing? What are you so desperately avoiding? But I think she understood, or would anyway, poor thing, the not-so-particular weirdness of my own heart, given a few good minutes snooping in my journal, if I'd bothered keeping one.

"I'll tell you why," I said. "I thought those implants were absolutely ridiculous. I mean to say, do you want a world full of people with eddy implants in their heads? I knew everyone would eventually want them. They were rather cool."

"Okay, so you thought it was ridiculous, and eddy didn't pursue it?" She seemed to find this improbable.

"I am a cofounder here," I reminded her. "Wade and I *were* partners. Granted, I didn't know what he was talking about most of the time. I'm not saying I couldn't have done better. Probably I could have. Probably you could have. Much better."

"Why do you keep talking about me like that? Who am I to you?"

"I don't have a crush on you, if that's what you mean."

To this she had no idea how to respond.

"I mean," I went on, "I'm not irrationally projecting attributes onto you. As a matter of fact, that's what Wade did to me. I abetted it. I took advantage. I didn't want the world to smother me like just anyone. Can you understand? I think so. Am I projecting?"

She considered. "No," she said.

"It is too bad how it went, but even before eddy there was all the same trouble. I just added the dead to it, really. I don't know if I would take that back. That's my one non-regret."

"Your *one* non-regret? You regret everything else?"

"Sure."

This pleased her. She smiled before remembering she was out to be sympathetic.

"Kindly refrain," I said, "from looking at me that way through those huge glasses, young lady. I'm a middle-aged man. It's not so unusual."

"Well, I'm glad you stopped the chips," she allowed. "That was good."

It made a difference to her, this chip thing.

"I only delayed them," I said. "I can't anymore. The rest of Executive doesn't see me quite the way Wade did."

"Huh. You are kind of a control-freak after all, aren't you?"

"You think you aren't?"

"Wait till you see what I'm demanding."

"Run it by me when you're done with a draft. I am curious."

"Fine. You know . . ." she started, looking at me in a new way. I tried not to look too different. I had wanted her to understand me a little, and she did.

"Yes?" I prompted.

"I think this might be good for you—except the starving part."

We both laughed. Even then, mortality seemed far off. I felt only relief, and perhaps she felt relieved. With her hair going every way, her magnified eyes easing from tension to fatigue, she looked like someone just deposited by a cyclone. I stopped myself from squeezing her shoulder or some such gesture. She turned deep orange and squinted. The sun had risen.

CHAPTER TWENTY-THREE

WE HADN'T FULLY SNUFFED out springtime. Wildflower flared through the meadows, from our heights not unlike a species of sunset, interrupted here and there by a clover of highway ramps. We had reached the outskirt of a picturesque American city reduced, however, to accepting the uproar of protests for the boon of corporate and diplomatic travel spending. No doubt the protestors and their military counterparts were also a sort of boon, eating and sleeping and buying lip balm as they must. We came to hover high over a tract of abandoned farmland, where we would remain throughout the summit. A cloud shadow strayed across and seemed to pause, sniffing at our tiny, doglike shadow, the four smaller gas bladders providing stumpy legs beneath the main, rounded belly. I turned over. The bleak underside of a cloud. Over. Down through the water the rainbow netting jittered, tracing new rhythms and structures, circuits connecting, disconnecting. At last, the din of rotors stopped. The exodus was complete.

Demands:

She had gotten that far since my last check. I watched my old foe drum it's thin, black finger at her. Finally, she added:

So the idea is, instead of taking individual power to break the system, pivot to handing the system the power to break you and kill you. So beautiful in its simplicity. Why didn't I think of this sooner?

Switching to eddyMessage, she hammered out:

H, should I assume the app update isn't coming? I'd really like to have that in my pocket if the strike doesn't catch on, which I realize is a strong possibility, and I've had no response at all from Fabio. Should I be worried that I haven't heard from you either?

Without sending, she returned, now more fluently:

How did Stoutmeier talk me into this? Because he was thinking of attainable demands. I'm still thinking symbolically, the grand demonstration. Balance emerging from individual inspiration, a functioning ecosystem. Okay, the current dysfunction could still make it easier, clear the way. They could possibly let us stay alive long enough to get rid of them. There you go, pragmatism, Z. Swallowing the pride, what's the ask? The minimum:

After a pause she amended: *The absolute minimum:*

She was on her way. I paddled to the landing, donned the worn slippers and arguably non-pajama bottoms, spiraled down, and set out wandering the yacht as if to convince myself that eddy was truly gone. To be left by a company, to leave a company, to leave a job—I almost wish I could give you, reader, an early-21st-century job if only to experience its remission. At eddy the work of course was mental, a shifting complex of cares not much connected to life, dominating life. Back then there was a disorder called schizophrenia, in which the sufferer spent his days under the strain of complicated, towering abstractions unrecognized by the rest of humanity. To feel that fall away, all that headless heap of projects, timelines, projections, tasks, lifted in a stroke, to be instantly cured, for this miracle it was almost worth getting hired to begin with.

Little as I had done of late, the disappearance of eddy, all those enduring madmen, was deeply liberating. I ran my hand over a strip of decorative moss and said, welcome back, welcome back! Passing the main pool, I was surprised to hear voices echoing from within.

A dozen leftover interns were gathered close on beach chairs, a bowl of pickled eggs on the tiles between them. It was still full, the dears. Against the bar, thoughtfully popping pretzels, leaned stout Jake, who I suppose would never have left the yacht while there was still fun to be wrung from it.

"Gandhi!" he called, catching sight of me. "Come."

The interns, turning, looked for a moment alarmed. One waved me over.

I couldn't say I had noticed any of these people before—no, a preposterously pretty, big-nosed girl had been the egret-like dj of the night before. They were all young women but one, or anyway this person wore short, parted hair and men's shoes. They were still dressed for their internships, though their talk had the unmeandering, self-excited tone of a recreational sports team crowding up to the bar in grass-stained uniforms. They had a right to be excited with themselves. They were the righteous few, whatever their motives. Why should they forget their image, their following? One had to make allowances for these rarefied souls, stars of social media before they knew they were alive, and then *brands*, or so the real brands would have it, the advertisement that swaddled them and must have been all but indistinguishable from the rest of reality, omnipresent, adapting, molding the image they had no chance to replace with themselves. Where could they find such a thing as themselves? Perhaps these too, talking revolution on white beach chairs, were newborns. Perhaps this lamentable generation was scratching away at the inside of its egg, pale beaks starting to break through.

"As you were," I said, pulling up a lounger. "Thank you. Please."

"Is Zoraida coming?" asked a young woman in an appetizing rainbow-sherbet designer button-up.

I was tickled to be thought of as an authority on Zoraida, and sorry that her duties deprived her of this companionable scene. No doubt she was really more content fretting away at our statement. I reclined, half-listening to the others in their resuming intensity—what their parents and teachers and friends would say, or had said, what they themselves would tell the world—and felt myself drowsing, drifting up into the folds of a cloud.

I shouldn't have noticed Zoraida looming over my lounger. The others went on, eyes closed, backs straight, minding their interiors. The headmistress hummed. She too was still among us. Hunting up a digestif, Jake had come upon her and Stoutmeier in a pantry, reportedly inventorying vegetables. Whether because he feared the interns were growing feeble with hunger or because he couldn't bear to not exert himself on the general experience, he convinced the sage to provide some basic instruction that might after all come in handy. Candles that should not have been allowed aboard burned on the turquoise tiles. The pool jets quietly plashed. Although a poor student of the art, I was enjoying the lesson, peeking around at the rest. Now I looked up dreamily at Zoraida, who had plainly not managed a nap. In her big glasses the dry eyes swam.

"I haven't been envying you," I whispered. "Have you had a smoothie? Please sit." I slid over a space on the padded white beach chair.

She didn't sit but handed me her eddy with an air of woe. I scrolled. I scrolled more. The bare minimum was not what I'd imagined.

"All of this?" I asked. "I think we might rather . . ."

She knew better than to wait. "Do you want me to read it to you?"

"You maybe meditate a bit. I'll read," I said quietly, and began. She watched.

The first items described protections for various groups of people. It all sounded to me like things that must have been already in place, but one is a white man in the sky. The environmental items struck me as less plausible—pages of points on farming, mining, clothing. There followed a versatile denunciation of our own executive, legislative, and judicial branches, with a list of hygienic prescriptions: we demanded that that the combined wealth of the Cabinet members not exceed that of the combined lower third of America. Corporations like eddy whose market capitalization exceeded the GDP of Mexico must recuse themselves from future global policy summits. Antibiotics here at home must be made financially feasible to sufferers of syphilis, strep throat, and much more. It was admirable, reasonable, and far too much, the world righted in ten typed pages.

"This is all wonderful," I whispered, "but I wonder if something more . . . more the spirit of the thing, less specific . . . catchier, if you will, a sort of rallying cry . . ."

"You mean vaguer? Why doesn't it surprise me you would want something vague? Vagueness is not inspiring. If you want to change the specifics, I'm listening."

"Can I talk to you out there for a moment?" I said gently. The meditators must have been pretending at this point.

"You're backing out," she said, no longer whispering. "Remember this morning. I warned you. You said—"

"No," I said, wronged at this ready loss of faith. Or, it struck me, was it possible she hoped, if only subconsciously, that I'd back out? Was this document engineered in part to ensure as much, letting her conscience off with having made the uncompromising, Zoraida-esque effort? Was part of her counting on me to save her? "I don't accept this," I said, attentive for betrayed relief.

She betrayed none, but snatched back the eddy, bleary eyes narrowing. I moved quickly to the exit. She followed, maintaining sufficient composure to not yell at my back until the stair door clicked behind us on the observation deck.

"*Coward.*"

I faced around, and, with a meekness that could only have been maddening, said, "This isn't going to be your only shot, Zoraida. You're going to be doing wonderful, admirable things for a long time."

"It's not *my* shot. It's got nothing to do with me. Didn't reading that give you at least some sense of what's happening on that little blue-green speck down there you might vaguely remember having lived on?"

"I meant you'll have a long life of doing things like this. There will be more to do. It would help if you were still here to do it."

Clamping hands to hips, as though holding herself down, she asked, "Do you honestly believe I'll be in a position anything like this again? Do you know how hard I worked to get a chance like this? I don't mean as an intern. You obviously realize by now I don't want a job at eddy. Do you know what the Earth is going to look like even if they do everything we're asking for in section two? Your beloved Earth?"

"I suppose taken as a percentage of your life, all that work seems a long time, but listen to an old man—"

"How old are you?"

"Forty-eight."

"*Forty-eight?* What's the life expectancy of a billionaire who drinks nothing but health smoothies in a giant climate-controlled bubble? Meanwhile, you guys don't even give us health insurance! My father died at thirty-nine. Taken as a percentage of my life, I'm probably older than you are. I already had a full-time job in high school. I'm not like those girls down there at the pool."

"I know," I said. "I was only saying you have a whole—"

"—life ahead of me. Wasn't it you who just made that speech? Do I *want* to spend the next fifty years working all day at some NGO where hundreds of us together barely make a dent in the most basic problems? Am I obligated to prefer a life of trifling-ass do-goodery and indignant letter-writing, and whatever ineffectual, ordinary, mind-numbing shit when I could do something actually significant, just *fucking* do it?"

"I understand," I said. I understood, not the heroism part, but the other part. I felt awfully sorry for her.

"I don't think you do," she said.

"Can we make a deal?"

"Absolutely not. No deal."

"I won't change a word," I said, "but you leave. You can wait until you're faint with hunger if you want, but eventually you have to leave."

This didn't seem to please her. Her mouth started to work as though in protest, and then, startlingly, crumpled. Behind the thick lenses her unblinking, exhausted eyes filled. It hadn't crossed her mind, or she hadn't let it cross her mind, that I, or maybe anyone, would concern themselves with her welfare.

"You poor, rich bastard," she said. I didn't see why.

"Deal?" I said.

"Fine," she said, wiping her cheeks with the flat of her hand.

Then I saw. She was concerning herself with my welfare. I would be staying, yes, but if I was taking her place at the stake, I was also dealing in pesos, lira, play money. I was no better able to picture real privation than the smoker pictures his future lung tumors, the drinker his liver transplant, the army enlister his dismemberment in a ditch. It was just like any pass we meet for lack of morbid imagination. I was far better equipped to picture ordinary days one after the next, which in fact I did as greyish freight cars repeating in file to the horizon, and I shuddered to be the continual coal shoveler of that overmatched engine.

Why shudder? My life was a dream, and it pained me, and in the moment I abandoned it to fate, it stopped paining me. I felt good, but not heroic. It was softer, subtler, paler, what I felt. It was maybe just company.

"Do you want to go read our demands to the others?" I asked.

"I guess I should give them a crack at it," she said. "I might have forgotten something."

This was a little joke, and she smiled. I looked up at the dispersing overcast, saving that smile in case I would need it.

CHAPTER TWENTY-FOUR

"I'll just read it to you guys," Zoraida said.

She stood by the makeshift bar, facing the small remainder of Sky Yachters, nested in cushions on the pool deck. Only Stoutmeier sat apart, soaking his feet in the shallow end, holding an unbitten pickle like a cigar.

"Item one," Zoraida began. She rested her weight on one leg, the other trailing behind in the way of ancient, long-toed statuary. I thought of "standing liberty" on the nineteenth-century silver dollars in which I had tried to take an interest during Wade's numismatics craze of the summer before third grade. "These basic protections for women's health and security must be enacted into law federally or in all states not already compliant with the following . . ."

She reeled off the improbable terms with such conviction, after each sub-item pausing to menace the audience with her gaze, that all the well-meaning interns could do was nod along, until at last the lone boyish person said, "Wait," and I saw trouble. This fellow at least had seen beyond the force and rightness of Zoraida's delivery to the difficulties, to what it would mean for him.

"Can you start again?" he asked, taking out his eddy. "Someone should be getting this."

"Fine. Ready?" Zoraida said. She paused, as if waiting for her new audience, the lawmakers, executives, whoever it was she imagined, to take their ghostly seats among us. When she resumed, her cheeks had flushed, not, however, as I first thought, with embarrassment, but with anger. Her voice quavered. Her dark eyes fixed on mine.

"You know what you've done. I won't tell you everything you'll do to fix it. I'm not trying to dictate a new way of life. That obviously starts without a dictator. I think it already has, inside many of us. I'm just telling you what has to happen now so that you have a chance in hell of living it."

After some hesitation, the interns clapped. I clapped.

"Okay, item one . . ." She went into it, now with complete self-possession, speaking slowly, even with a measure of charm, like a schoolteacher who after scaring the bejesus out of her students lets them see she's still with them at heart.

The lone boy was right. Even getting item one for the third time in the hour, I was drawn in, much as back when trying to take an adolescent interest in football, flipping between games I would get sucked into the whirl of a figure skater out there before the masses, as if the hours she'd spent so maniacally dreaming this moment had accreted to it an inviolate gravitational field. So I pictured Zoraida down in her Baltimore bedroom fulminating to her imagined audience, all of those speeches, the force of all that lonely devotion pushing forward, turning those imaginary listeners into ourselves.

She managed not to smile through the applause at the end. Did anyone have anything to add? The hands of Stoutmeier and the headmistress shot up, and I stole away, wanting to preserve a while longer my giddy sensation of having been dreamed, together with all those who would see the footage, years ago in dingy solitude behind a lighted window anyone at all might have walked past.

CHAPTER TWENTY-FIVE

WHITE SWIRLED UP FROM the west as though just poured into the blue saucer of sky. It was the diaphanous, color-catching film you want at this altitude, but at the last moment all was lost, as are so many such sunsets, snuffed by a thicker cloud at the very horizon. Zoraida surfaced.

"This damn cloud on the horizon," I observed. "I may have to ask Goldfarb to raise us back up just for the hour."

"They might be disappointed," she said, looking down over the rail.

In the pasture below were news vans, at some distance from each other but all facing the same way, like lions at a watering hole. A number of other cars were parked closer to the road. From one of them a family walked into the field, joining a group gathered on the grass beneath our bow. I took them for Sky Yacht gawkers on their way to or from the protests downtown, as several held signs. The arrivals now began unrolling a large picnic blanket, which kept going unreasonably, as though for a banquet. This too turned out to be a sign, now legible. It said, "Look up!" I looked up. Blue drained to grey. The imp of a round pink cloud gazed down.

"Do you see anything?" I asked Zoraida.

She laughed. "They're just protesting with us."

"Oh, did the statement go out already?"

"Bob is still editing a few of the videos together. Those are your people. He must have posted a clip from your insane address last night."

"What do you think they mean, look up?"

"That was your own line!" She laughed again. She was in much the best mood I'd seen from her. "It's a good line. *Catchy.*"

"I do recall babbling that somewhere in there."

"I think you're partly faking it, by the way, all this vagueness. Appealing to my colleagues' social media dreams was a pretty shrewd maneuver if you ask me."

"My success rate was fairly low, but I think the ones who stayed are sincere, in a way. How did they react to the demands? Was there any trouble? I snuck out right after the reading."

"Bob and Gloria had a lot to say, but just particulars. It's all right. The others threw in a few little things, just to feel like they were involved. They weren't upset, if that's what you mean. I think they actually believe it's going to work out. When have these people not achieved something? Success is all they know."

"I suppose she who really has mortality moaning in the marrow isn't a twenty-something Ivy Leaguer with an elite business internship."

"Yeah. Not like us misfits," she said, to my delight. "I think they do mean well, but they'll find a way to leave at some point without their conscience exactly roasting them. They'll have done more than most, and it will be time for them to think about their families, and all that shit."

"As it will be for you. We have a deal."

"Till the last minute. I want to be already passed out. Then I guess I can't stop you from evacuating me."

We were quiet for a moment, affected by this vision.

"It is a pity," I said, "you didn't have more time to take advantage of the cuisine. A month or two in that dining hall could have done much for your reserves."

She stepped toward me—close enough that my heart went backward—and took hold of my upper arm.

"Ow!"

She'd pinched me.

"Is that reserves?" she said. "You're going to pass out first is what I think. Don't worry, I'll go ahead and evacuate you at the first sign of malaise. Then we might even have a chance here. Sorry, it's a weird reverse gender thing, but there's a reason why Berkman was maligned even by the workers he sacrificed himself for while Emma was beloved."

I tried to look substantially blanker than might one who had just read this in her Humans application essay.

"Do you not know about this?" she said, aghast. "Alexander Berkman and Emma Goldman tried to kill the steel tycoon Henry Clay Frick?"

"Oh, yes. I love the Frick. Fragonard . . ."

"Jesus Christ."

"Wait, am I Berkman or Frick in this scenario?"

She thought about it. "A little of both."

Berkman and Emma Goldman, I recalled from my brief further research, had been lovers. Perhaps this fact had surfaced in Zoraida's mind too, because next she said, "Why don't you really have a girlfriend, or a boyfriend? At this point you can't tell me you aren't lonely."

"Why doesn't everyone?"

"I don't because I don't believe in hierarchical relationships, monogamy, all that heteronormativity. Neither did Emma, for that matter. Is that your reason?"

"No."

"I didn't think so. Was it because of Wade Aubrey? You said something about that. You were taking advantage of his attachment. You were afraid if you had someone else he would stop doting on you, get rid of you? Was he in love with you?"

"I suppose I did worry how it would make him feel."

"Seriously? You consigned yourself to a life of loneliness and I'm guessing severe sexual deprivation just to be nice?"

In fact I hadn't meant to be a monk. Like so much in life, it came down to a failure of morbid imagination in the crucial moment. The sky. Swimming pools. Close quarters with all sorts of clever people. I didn't occur to me that eddy *power dynamics* would render everyone in sight, preposterously, my inferior, out of bounds. And the sorts of clever people weren't my sort.

"Well," I said, "what are the options? There are the education people, but they switch out most flights and most of the time are kids."

"No wonder you're so obsessed with that earth-body fascist." Zoraida still didn't like the headmistress. "Not to mention clouds. This can't be healthy."

"I'm really all right," I laughed, embarrassed. I was all right. I felt splendid.

"Look, Mr. Curtis," she said. "For this part, I mean . . . your part, would you rather stick to being lonely—would that be easier? Or would you rather not be?"

"It might be easier," I considered. "No I wouldn't rather. No."

She nodded. "We could pass out together, a dead tie. Then what? Where will we even be after the summit?"

"With eddy's commitments, we never had time to go very far north. If you can believe it, I've never seen the aurora borealis."

"You think you'll last that long, do you? How fast could this thing get there from here?"

"Just a few weeks. Six, seven."

Zoraida made her face look encouraging, as I must have lately made my face look encouraging at Wade's bedside, listening to his grand futures.

"Good thing," she said, "we've screwed up the ionosphere to the point where I'm pretty sure you can see them from Vermont on a good day. I wouldn't scoff at some northern lights at the end of the tunnel, myself. Yeah. I would love that."

"What would you say," I said, "to a little smoothie right now? With ice cream I suggest, if that doesn't violate the sumptuary laws."

"All right," she said. "This sunset is below our standards anyway."

CHAPTER TWENTY-SIX

AS IT HAPPENED, THE others were already in the famous kitchen, smaller and steelier than I'd imagined it, upending cartons of coconut cream, water chestnut milk, cashew butter, those strawberries shaped like geodesic domes, lettuces, taut grapes, and withered mummies of ginger and turmeric into blenders. We carried the beige product out to the dining hall, where Stoutmeier and Gloria, the headmistress, waited under the chandelier's high crystal rapids, absorbed in news.

The journalist looked up at the arriving company and our frothy pitchers with the air of an embattled army officer sizing up a busload of scrawny, squinting recruits.

"It's started down there," he briefed us. "Two protestors shot, one crushed." His tone was grave, censorious, and boastful. "The story is they were shot by other protestors. Four officers critically injured. These are just the opening skirmishes. Wait till tomorrow. You people—"

"Bob, enough," said the headmistress, laying a hand on the pilled sweater. "There's also this," motioning us in and turning the eddy around so we could see.

The Sky Yacht lurked in twilight above a newswoman asking a man in the crowd, which looked bigger than it had from above, "What brings you out here tonight?"

"I wanted to support the strikers," the man replied blandly. "And I wanted to show my son."

A seven-year-old gaped up at us.

"We're getting some *love*," observed the egret girl. "I want to see them."

The interns started up for the observation deck.

"Maybe leave the smoothies," Stoutmeier said coolly.

The world was not meant to know about the smoothies.

The news footage must have been broadcast on a delay, for there was little to see. Spots of eddy light moved along the pasture toward the road, where headlights came on and crept away. The news vans remained, but darkened. No one had turned on the deck lights, as it happened, so we too were in darkness.

"*Oh*," someone said.

I knew that oh. It was the wondering vocal vapor trail of a really good shooting star. The sky was mostly clear and our eyes were well dilated from scrutinizing the pasture. The moon had yet to make a mess of things. Like mist down the middle sprawled the Milky Way, and you could see the slight blues and oranges of the young and waning stars. Considering the proximity of the town, it was a very starry night, though little enough compared with the prehistoric celestial bath of a mile or two up, in which you might as easily draw constellations from the dark spots. Even before Jake's evening reign, stargazing was never a big occupation of the interns, and those remaining were unspoiled by their week aloft. They craned back, mouths pulled open by the angle, like the recent seven-year-old, or like themselves as children stepping out of the car after the long Friday-night drive to the country house. Someone lay down on the deck, hands under head. The rest of us followed, lying full out.

Besprinkled lightyears from cheekbone to brow were interrupted only by the shaft of the upper pool and its encircling spiral stair, reaching away starkly black. At first there was some unfortunate talk of the constellations. Someone knew Cassiopeia, someone knew the Seven Sisters, but eventually the general sense of having shown up unprepared for a pop quiz subsided. A blanket lofted and sank over me. A few people were going around covering the stargazers, two or three to a blanket. I'd hardly noticed the body heat I'd been losing to the floorboards, but now the blanket was delicious. It twitched. Zoraida had put her knees up. She had been so quiet, or I had become so accustomed to watching the sky with her, I had forgotten she was there.

As the warmth oozed down my nerves, I sent myself back to the night after Wade's funeral, watching the stars from my hammock and listening to the companionable din of the new interns, imagining their conversations like a spirit trying to reconstruct from fading memory the nostalgic particulars of life. Now I raised my head to take in the fellow gazers, soundless, as though muffled by the blankets, or connected by them in a medium in which sound was superfluous. The next meteor I spotted, a small one, no vapor trail, directly above, others must have seen. Ten minutes passed before the next, a huge greenish streaker down half the sky, and again not a sound.

There was, actually, some light snoring. And then, perhaps gently shaken by a neighbor, a pitchy figure stood, depthless black, like a human hole in the sky, and moved off. One by one they stole away, mindful of the enchantment, or still under it, always after a star fell, having kept some pact with themselves. Maybe they'd been making wishes. Clouds of sleep drifted through me, bringing and carrying away strange portents. I woke with aching shoulder blades and sacrum.

It was my usual waking hour. In the wan predawn light I saw the deck broad and empty but for Jake, on his side, hands together childlike under his sleeping Newfoundland face, and Zoraida, very straight under the blanket, like Snow White in her casket. I stood painfully, a poor attempt at stealth. She woke, looked around confused, looked at me confused. She stood, wrapping the blanket around her, and walked sleepily to our spot at the rail.

CHAPTER TWENTY-SEVEN

PALTRY RED FADED OVER cheap subdivisions. Already cars were parked in the road alongside our pasture, early birds rolling out blankets under our bows. I'd gotten as far as "Goldfarb, raise us just a minute—" before finding I didn't feel especially deprived. I suppose I felt alive, in the way people mean when they say they feel alive. The timing could have been better. Maybe it's only when you know you're selling the windy old estate that you can finally afford to turn on the furnace. Ah but then how warm it seems.

"Never mind, Goldfarb. Let them have us."

Zoraida and I dispersed to our respective quarters to wash up and change for the day, and I did even briefly wash before checking her eddy. She was reading:

> Z—Sorry for the delayed response. We've seen your "demands" video and Bob Stoutmeier's write-up in the Times.
>
> While we applaud the intention, we're concerned that you didn't consult us, and we thank you for not mentioning the organization in anything else you may disseminate. We've discussed and think it best at this time to sever our association. I'm sorry, but our position remains that the original plan is of vital significance, not only to show global capital/mind-control

that it's deeply vulnerable, but to show those they oppress the power each holds as an individual. The identity of the individual was never meant to be important. This was not about your own personal glory or martyrdom.

Of further concern is that the participation of Chris Curtis complicates and weakens this protest you've elected to stage in place of what we meticulously planned, and for which we've paid for your schooling over the past year. We do hope, however, that you're enjoying your millions of views and that the attention satisfies the craving that drove you to this, or to activism in general.

Please don't try to contact Fabio again. He hasn't shown up in three days, and we're no longer interested in supporting him either.

Yours regretfully,
H

Before I had reached the bottom, Zoraida was bashing out her reply:

To whom it may CONCERN,

I hope severing with me restores your illusion of having had any part in this plan beyond paying for a year of education which frankly was not the make-or-break factor. I think you know that I would have gotten myself in this position regardless. I do thank you for offering the apparently phony moral support I admit I needed back when I, a teenager, brought you, established supposed adults, your big idea. It had been my dream, not yours, to see the Sky Yacht raining down like a weeping willow firework on the plutocrats' heads. If empathy was more than a buzzword with you, you might stop to imagine the difficulty of giving that up for something more arduous and productive.

Z

P.S. - You should have been nicer to Fabio.

P.P.S. - You're just a disgusting human being.

This last postscript she immediately erased, and she still hadn't sent the message when I switched to camera to find myself already in a pocket. I rinsed my mouth with searing purple and dashed back up to the sunrise.

Zoraida watched the crowd gathering on the grass below with an air of preoccupation. It infected me. In my satisfaction over the peaceful evolution of her schemes, and the success of my own, in the companionable smoothies and stargazing, the disappearance of all the official people and their oppressive cares, I had neglected the danger of her case.

Clearly this Fabio fellow had informed whatever governmental agency it was of the Humans' plans to destroy the yacht above the summit, though I was sure he hadn't identified Zoraida to them any more than he had to us, had tattled as much out of concern for his Dulcinea as for the rest of us and perhaps the whole world. But unless she had really been incredibly careful, the government would connect her with the group before long. They might have been content to let it slide had she and her Humans managed to keep eddy from making our play at the summit. Instead of that, she had produced a viral video denouncing them, and I couldn't imagine she'd be left to her leisure here if this small crowd beneath us developed into anything like the crowd already being cudgeled, or, as they say, controlled, a few miles east in the city center.

A banner, newly laid out on the rim of the settlement, read in huge block letters *We ♥ Zoraida*.

"Ah, celebrity culture," I said appreciatively.

This she ignored. Her mouth hung in an incipient smile or grimace. Her eyes were wet.

Abashed, I said, "I'm glad to have known you before you were inured to this sort of thing. It is surreal."

It soon got more so. By the time I sent Zoraida off to spy on her, half of the pasture was occupied. What at dawn had been a lazy, patchwork cloud in a green sky had become a thunderhead in which only the variations among jackets, hats, and tilting sign boards traced, like sunset along the storm's underside, an unsuspected confederacy of colors.

> It would be convenient not to be seething with hatred right now. I know there's something I'm not seeing. Focus, Z. If you can spare a brief intermission in the inner Helen tirade, like I have something to prove to her. Jesus. What does that letter actually mean? I would almost think they're planning to forge ahead, and that the disgustingly inhuman tone after all this time is Helen convincing herself that I'm a person it's okay to blow up for the general good. Could the app work from down there? Could they get it together to launch something at us? They might not dare over a whole field of peaceful protestors. If she hadn't cursed me I really would be relishing these people, and honestly my view count as well. I'm not

here to pretend I didn't spend years fantasizing about this. To finally do something that's even noticeable, that anyone actually cares about. That goddamn sign they rolled out. It's harder than I fantasized though, keeping this from your heart. Maybe it's best someone takes me out before I become a crazed despot. Maybe we can still do a ceremonial explosion of the yacht in the end. That would be joyous, I have to say. I'm developing a weirdly upbeat idea that we're all going to survive this in some non-disgraceful way. Someone will probably come pick up Curtis at some point whether he likes it or not. I don't think they let billionaires starve to death even if they want to.

CHAPTER TWENTY-EIGHT

FROM THE GROUND, AS seen on Stoutmeier's eddy, our crowd looked in fine form. "What's their goal?" it called. "Control!" it responded. "Un-hook yourself!" it called. "Look, yourself!" it responded. The cadence I found grating, but I was impressed with individual specimens. Many were schoolchildren. My favorite, before the coverage cut away from her, was a young girl departing from the call-and-response to gleefully bellow, "We're all going to die!" Here now was a vigorous elderly woman with a sign reading *HEY PLUTOCRACY: ENOUGH ALReddy*. A college-age boy held up a depiction of the Sky Yacht, foreshortened such that the main egg projected phallically above testicular rear gas bladders, with the script *STAY HARD*. Here was a fine trio of fellows without signs, in glasses and cashmere scarves. Above the crowd, kids on shoulders bounced to the chant, young fathers holding a colorful rain boot in each hand. Consuming much of our view of this scene was a stream of very short messages from all over the world, a barely intelligible barrage of @s and #s and cartoonish symbols which apparently contributed in some vital way to the value of the news. These dispatches seemed anyway to be an exuberant comment on the scene, some perhaps from the participants themselves. They were united by the *tag*, or organizing principle, *#lookup!*

Back on deck, the ex-interns hunched over what might still be called, if it's possible it ever really was called, *oak tag*, painting protests of their own. Below, buses discharged arrivals into the crowd that now extended to the verge of the surrounding woods on the port side, for hundreds of yards of pastureland around the protuberance of the Sky Yacht belly sternward, and out to the forested strip that hid the highway on the bow side, beyond which lay the city. A looser crowd formed on the far side of the local road to starboard. I felt a throb of vertigo. It all seemed out of hand, precarious, primally unnerving.

"It's wonderful, isn't it?" I said to Zoraida, who again looked more preoccupied than pleased. "It's catching on."

"I don't know," she said. "Emma Goodman said no good ever came from the mass. That's starting to look like a mass to me. It is painful to hold yourself back from it, that big old hug, I know, but if you don't want to be manipulated, a good rule of thumb is to not repeat after some guy with a megaphone whatever a thousand other people are chanting all around you with their fists raised. It sounds so right. It feels good. We're built to just soak this in. It's a party. It's family. What could go wrong?"

"The cynicism, Zoraida. They're chanting for us."

"People chant. Have you ever seen a rally during primary season? It's a lot louder than this, and for what? Some random guy crawls out of the woodwork with enough cash to make himself seem legit, and a couple months later millions of people across the country show up chanting his name like a bunch of Aztecs at a volcano. No rock star ever had it so good as this bald scion in a Brooks Brothers tie. And then we get mad at what happens next. It's like yelling at your kid for being class clown when you serve him white Russians for breakfast."

"It is remarkable," I agreed, "the humility, the hope. I am at best an amateur egoist, but I don't think I would have it in me to go chant someone else's name in a crowd of people doing the same for hours on end. I think it's touching. The selflessness, the readiness to band together. We really are a people of deepest humility and hope."

"Jesus Christ, Chris."

"Aren't you the one who loves humanity?"

"That's why it *infuriates* me. If I didn't I would sound like you."

"What do I sound like?"

"A priest-for-hire at a funeral."

"You know, Zoraida, something's going to make you happy sometime and you'll be lost."

Her eyes widened. "Something's going to wake *you* up from total anesthesia sometime and you'll be a *disaster*. I might do it myself."

"Are we about to burst into a musical number?"

Aggressively staring, she did a little tap step. I envied her energies.

"I really am not used to spending so much time upright," I said. "I'm going to my pool for a little."

"All right," she said. "But I have to go down and change."

"What?"

"I asked and you said you'd rather not be alone. Right?"

I laughed. I was moved. "I'll be all right for a bit. You don't have to."

"Hey, it's not every day you get asked to the top VIP pool on the goddamn Sky Yacht. There are whole albums written about this shit."

"You really do feel you're floating in the sky," Zoraida observed. "Except for that stupid antenna."

"Yes, my old nemesis. I wonder if at this point I could get rid of it. What would happen?"

"Eventually you'd crash into something. That's the IoT receiver." Perhaps belatedly registering the improbability of this detailed Sky Yacht knowledge, she added, brightly, "Maybe paint it blue?"

I looked at the intern, supine on a second float I'd scrounged up, wearing the red two-piece familiar from the Palmer-throttling footage, ankles crossed, one hand resting on her stomach. I rolled back to the sky, feeling pleasantly vaporous. High above, ponds of blue shone here and there in the grey-white dishevelment. Off-zenith southward, uneven overcast reeled past the sun.

"It is a pity about the altitude," I complained. "The key, during these floats, is to be *amongst* the clouds, yet without being inside any particular one for too long, where of course it's just white. Then the pockets of blue become the pool we're in, and the white other splendid worlds."

I had often enough addressed such analyses to the ghost of someone or other beside me.

"I see," said Zoraida. Mimicking my tone, "*Secret caves rugged and dark, their starry domes of diamond and of gold expanding above numberless and immeasurable halls, frequent with crystal column?*"

"That too," I said.

If I had gotten a bit lyrical, I hadn't meant to propose myself as a competitor to Shelley.

But she continued, more charitably, "*Nor had that scene of ampler majesty than gems or gold, the varying roof of heaven and the green earth lost in his heart its claims to love and wonder.*"

"Ah," I said. "Exactly. Thank you. What is that? *The Spirit of Solitude* again?"

"*Again?*" She craned up to squint at me.

"I mean," I scrambled, pulse jumping a register, "that first bit was surely *The Spirit of Solitude.*"

She subsided onto the float. "It's the one poem I have memorized. I loved that poem. I'm surprised you're not more familiar."

"I'm vaguely familiar," I said vaguely.

"Anyway," she said, "after the summit, we'll be back *amongst.*"

Yes we would. I put my hands behind my head and sighed up at the blue patches. Perhaps this was how it felt, after all, to be rich. A vee of Canada geese flew overhead, incurious, northward. I either dreamed or actually saw Jake's shaggy head rise and slip back under, grinning. Off to the east, a single slanting sun ray descended from heaven like an ironic drawbridge to downtown Charlotte and slowly swept our way. In the moment of intersection, we flipped over to watch the light's maniacal rainbow jitterbug on the pool floor, which was both fast and slow, like the days of life, and was gone.

CHAPTER TWENTY-NINE

A THIN OVERCAST MOUNTED up from the horizon like a windshield half-smashed, branched cracks holding the last sun. The crowd covered the pasture.

"Here they come," said Zoraida.

I hadn't noticed much riot police, though no doubt they had been accumulating in step with the crowd. Now a line of cruisers and a few bigger vehicles double-parked in the narrow road.

"Just protocol," I suggested. "There are an awful lot of people down there. And it's getting dark." I didn't like it. "When do you suppose all these people will go home?"

"I think they're camping. At least I hope they are," she added, perhaps remembering that these good folk with luck stood between ourselves and a plan-b attempt from her superiors. "I'm getting a lot of messages back from people who even claim to be fasting."

That gave me a pang. I imagined a waterslide-size crazy-straw conveying smoothie down to the faithful, the sort of Sky Yacht-esque idea I would have mentioned to Wade alone.

Along the verge of the road, armored officers lined up shoulder-to-shoulder behind their shields.

"Do we have lights we could aim down?" Zoraida asked. "Landing lights?"

"We'd have to get closer."

"We should. We should light up as much as we can, and we should be recording these guys."

"Goldfarb," I said. "Can you lower us, slowly, if you please—I don't want people thinking we're falling on them—and turn on the landing lights? Do we have cameras pointing down? I suppose we must. How else would you see anything? Make sure they're recording."

The lights came on below, picking up previously unsuspected mist, and we began to descend. Flashes popped from the twilit pasture. To those earthly photographers we must have looked as a bathysphere slowly falling through the fathoms, lights ablaze, looks to the strange, stunned creatures of the sea floor. The event, however, rather than the eerie spectacle, was the concern. The Sky Yacht had at last come within camera range, and this must be shared with the living, the dead, the yet unborn. By the time we stopped at a few hundred feet, the flashes were fizzing over the grey field like a vast electrocution, or some private retinal derangement that meant you were about to faint or travel through time. On that scale, the frantic, random pattern of light was disorienting, thrilling. Zoraida hadn't once looked away through the minutes of our descent. She was a girl alive to the visible world, but I had never seen her so transfixed by anything in the sky. The fine hair on her nape stood. She wiped her eyes. At last, then, through this stupendous display, the scope of what she'd started had penetrated her cynicism, or so I thought, but what she said, with a surprising break in her voice, was, "Sorry. It's just a de ja vu."

I didn't understand. I didn't push. I studied the now distinguishable crowd and the troops massed along the road with their shields and visors. After a moment, she continued on her own.

"When I was little," she said, "we lived for a few months in a sort of hillbilly town in Maryland. On the Fourth of July, my mom wanted to go to a party or something and my dad was supposed to take me to see the fireworks. Maybe he was afraid of parking or getting stuck in traffic with that crazy car of his. When I got in, he blindfolded me with his sweaty bandana. After like half an hour we stopped and he led me out of the car. I take off the bandana, and we're just parked at this random corner a few blocks from where we started—I had walked by it plenty of times. There was a run-down house and kind of a swampy overgrown yard, just total dereliction. And I thought, this is bad, something bad is about to happen. I was looking at the house, it was all dark. Suddenly the air starts to sparkle. Everywhere, like flashbulbs, on the ground, in the air, all through the trees, up to the very tops, thousands. I had seen plenty of fireflies, those yellow ones that zip up like soda bubbles from the ground at dusk. These were blue, and popping everywhere in space. My eyes were so dilated from the drive with the blindfold, I could see parts of the branches lighting up with each flash. The woods around the yard formed a sort of amphitheater. My dad was very proud of all this, like he had made it himself. He said this was what it looked like right at the start of a basketball game, or a huge rock concert, when the star comes out. See, Zora, you're a star. Right now only they know it, but you're going to be a star. He talked like that. The next summer we were in Baltimore, but even when I've been in the country I've never seen anything like that again, that one random corner with my dad. Till now." She paused. "Sorry," she said. "I know it's just chance, but there are moments when it's especially hard to be a rationalist. Do you know what I mean?"

It had yet to happen to me, but I was ready to believe that at least once in life such things are granted a person, a private wink from the universe, whether playful or spiteful.

I said softly, "I think he would say he was right."

She shrugged. "The weirdest thing is that I was just asking his emu the other day if he remembered it. Of course he didn't. See, I do talk to his emu. Sorry I was a dick about that before."

"How old were you?"

"When he died? Fourteen."

I nodded. I saw poor Zoraida at the graveside, her sad, kid eyes hardening.

"I was about that age when my mother died," I confided.

"I know," she said. "That's part of the emu creation myth, isn't it?"

"I suppose it is. What struck me was the time element. I didn't have to think of her as sick like I had for so long. Her sickness was just as gone as her healthiness. Suddenly, in a snap, both of those times, all of her times, were equally valid. That was the idea for the emu. Just loosening the tyranny a little."

And yet in all this time I hadn't had the nerve to resurrect the healthy woman or the sick woman who had been my mother. I wasn't sure my heart would bear her voice, that's true, but it was my own voice I feared more, to hear myself tell her who the boy she knew, with all his standard, limitless childhood magic, had become. Not that it was so dreadful what I'd become. But it was somehow, maybe for its sheer particularity—the impoverishment of all possibility to *this*—distasteful. And I could not have told her I was happy. That too maybe is nothing beyond the old human condition, but I sometimes wondered if she herself had left me available to a quality or intensity of loneliness others didn't feel. How could one know? Unless by spying. Zoraida was such good company because I saw, what I might never have from her presentation, that she felt it too, or something close. Suddenly we were pressed together. Jake had come from behind, ensausaging us with drunken force in his arms, saying something about confetti.

"I mean a *lot*," he said, "for the parties that won't be happening now. Let's dump it."

"I don't know if that's quite the note," I said. I glanced at Zoraida, mashed up to me. "We're not celebrating yet."

"We have to give them something," he insisted. "Look at them. They love us. Confetti from way up here. It'll be beautiful, sifting down, sifting . . . Picture it. They'll never forget. What do *you* say, cloud intern?"

"Let's save it for the right moment, I think."

It was unclear whether Jake processed this. Our constriction intensified, pinning us to his medial expanses like people testing a mattress. "I see you two talking," he said. "Now don't you go anywhere. I see things. We're just starting up here. Wait till bedtime."

We tried to show each other our bemusement, but now he had us by the wrists, raising them victoriously overhead like a boxing referee who couldn't bear to see either side lose. Something came over the crowd. It reminded me of the sudden textural transformations seen in camouflaged octopi, the sea floor suddenly coming alive. A thousand hands raised, and even through the dome the cheer was audible. Stoutmeier, whom we found just behind us, was *live-streaming* the moment to the multitudes. Hands waved and dropped. Here and there along the roadside a trooper's head, turning visored gaze upward, became pure light.

Thugs, the former interns called the riot police. Everyone was on deck now, excited, tipsy. *Shit* was about to *go down*. Already, so they told me, clashes between protestors—pro-Egarp, pro-Egal, anti-both, Green Roaders, and other factions whose names flew by me—had resulted in six fatalities around the conference center, clashes with troops another five, and hundreds dragged, dripping and roughed up, into detention at a disused middle school. In our pasture all looked peaceful enough. The crowd-control officers, through the little-used deck telescope, could be seen talking with their officer neighbors, with protestors, munching energy bars, laughing, furtively eddying.

The headmistress glided by, dead sober. I took this for another manifestation of her unimprovable interior, but, pressed by Jake's magnanimity, she explained. This headmistress of ours had been, as readers of her work well knew, an addict, and even a dealer. She had convened her first meditation group to cultivate well-heeled customers, who would like to feel that their habit was part of a regimen of the spiritual and exploratory. It still astounded her, the path by which she found her calling. Again I was ashamed for all the internal harangues I had given this woman. After all this time I still constantly underestimated the complications and troubles. Watching the interns, now cross-legged in a circle, I wondered what abuses even these diamantine strivers—so ideally clever, confident, concrete—might have suffered, what ghostly laurels, unsuspected even by themselves, hung over their hearts.

"Should we let them get some sleep down there?"

"It looks all right," Zoraida judged.

"Goldfarb, you can switch off the lights."

Instantly the field went out, and above the trees stars shone. The overcast had stealthily gone, and the sky, again moonless, seemed to fill second by second. I joined the mass on the floor, facing up.

"Look," said Zoraida beside me. Something on her eddy.

"No."

"Just look."

"I don't want to contract my pupils. Can you just describe it?"

"Fine. I told them all we're stargazing up here. I told them to watch with us for the first shooting star."

"Ah. Good. Very good."

"Think of all those people down there, watching the sky with you. How does it feel?"

"Wonderful," I said, trying to sound grateful and in fact deeply moved by the effort. "I feel like the prong at the center of a giant satellite dish."

CHAPTER THIRTY

ALREADY SORE FROM THE previous night's stargaze, my poorly padded shoulder blades roused me before midnight. The stars had shifted overhead, and a nearly full moon blotted the southeast sky. Close around, the interns lay like littermates, asleep or passed out. I sat. Zoraida's eyes reflected the moon.

"You're up?" I whispered. "I'm going in. I'm not very well cushioned, as a person."

"Okay," she said.

I got up. She stood too. All my life I had uneventful dreams, poignant nonetheless for their atmosphere of ease and belonging which was so plainly my true life that waking seemed more a return to the senseless exile of sleep. So smooth a continuation of the night's dreamlike accord was our walk to my room that it was a moment before I remembered, outside the door, to panic.

"Do you have a couch or something?" she asked, to my great relief and disappointment.

"You don't really have to be my shadow like this," I said. "I won't quit. I mean the strike."

"*Shadow?*"

"Not shadow, exactly. I mean . . ."

"You know you're not so special."

"I do know."

"You don't actually get to have a monopoly on everything."

"You don't understand."

"I do. You do. Enough vagueness. Look at me." I understood. She didn't want to be alone in this either. "Okay?" she said. "Can we go back to sleep now?"

Armchairs, sofa, dresser, and table were just inferable under strewn clothes, towels, notebooks, water bottles, ceramics, unhung paintings, dead plants, coils of never-used fairy lights. The floor too was only suggestion. Here and there from the sediments rose all but inaccessible stacks of books. Only my bed was reasonably clear, an unmade tangle of velvety, visibly unclean blankets, among which lazed large and small ancient stuffed animals. It had gotten bad. At first I had not liked the idea of having a maid, and things gradually reached the point where it would have been unconscionable. I intended to clean—I despise living in disorder—but at any moment I lacked the fortitude to begin. My quarters were a mountain, a monument of tedium. I spent as little time as possible here.

Zoraida took it in with an impressed whistle.

"I didn't expect," I said. "I've been meaning to. Et cetera. You take the bed. I'll take the hammock out there."

"Do you have any shorts I could borrow?"

"What you see," I said, sweeping a hand over my domains.

She stepped one by one out of her canvas shoes and tiptoed into the flotsam. At a stack of books she paused.

"*Moby Dick*," she said.

The top volume. I had reread it lately in anticipation of the book club I meant to start with Jake. She picked it up and, strangely, smelled the pages.

"Who's Ahab?" she asked.

"The mad captain."

"I know who Ahab is, you dickhead. I mean who's Ahab on the Sky Yacht?"

I thought for a moment. "You, I suppose."

She looked bemused, but said, "I'll take that. Stub?"

"Jake, obviously."

"Obviously. Starbuck?"

"Palmer," we said together.

I felt a little uncomfortable invoking Palmer under the circumstance, but it didn't seem to register anything with her. I suppose we weren't in competition.

"What about you?" she said. "Who are you?"

We thought about it, too long. I wasn't pleased to be negligible beyond all analogy.

"I know," she said. "The Parsee."

Ahab's spectral companion and shaman. Yes. I had been the Parsee from the Sky Yacht's very start.

"Zoraida! How are these shorts?" I cried, lofting the blue-green article her way.

"Just till I fall asleep, if you can spare it," she said. "Two minutes."

In the dark, prepared to lie like a slab on bed's edge for one hundred and twenty seconds, actually counting, I felt a hand grip my arm. I understood at once that she was offering, and asking, only comfort, in the shared peril I had not liked to think so grave, and submitted.

To the reader who hasn't taken the trouble to forever simulate with his own forearms another human's chest pressed to his, I would almost recommend it. The softness it was especially, the sinking softness of even so hard-looking a person, I'd forgotten. And the heat, which seemed to join that now pouring from some interior reservoir beneath my skin. We lay somewhat awkwardly clenched, and I don't think it would have been so amiss if, eyes closed and glaciers cleaving, our lips searched. I was not really quite a eunuch, and I don't say I didn't feel the stir, but it flew past my loins to my last lamented fibers, and such was the relief of this embrace that like a marathoner stopping at last to be swaddled in the shining mylar cape, I caught my breath and dropped instantly off to dreams.

Widows, widowers, numberless blue-lit homunculi, youths in your famed wireless virginities, all my dear unsung isolates, what a moment awaits you!

I woke in daylight, still clothed, clutching something to my chest. It was Zoraida's forearm. She lay looking at the ceiling, on which was painted a fresco of the sky. I had asked the artist to make it unclear whether the cloudlike polar bears were flying up to heaven or plummeting onto the viewer, but it didn't really come off. They looked merely suspended, startled.

"Sorry," I said, relinquishing the arm. "We missed sunrise."

"Just slightly. It's eleven-thirty. I guess you needed it."

"My God. How long have you been up?"

I rose, taking a moment to balance till the dark swarm cleared. Zoraida gave a yawning stretch. The best-maintained path in the place led from bed to window. I took it. My room was at the bow, which now faced the city. The sky was naked blue and hazed at the horizon. Below, signs thrust high, the multitude moved, I couldn't imagine where. Maybe they were just circumambulating the pasture to feel they were marching. I hoped the crowd-control officers had at least been spelled in the night. The field on the far side of the road was fuller than it had been.

"More supporters today," I reported back to Zoraida, who stood incautious of the dark swarm and toppled, landing seated on the floor.

She groaned. "I guess I'll get used to this," she said, rising again, gingerly.

"More riot police too," I said. The file of officers now stretched two-deep the length of the field.

Zoraida didn't reply. She was lost in her eddy.

"Bad news?"

"It's terrible downtown," she said voicelessly, forehead contracted.

"Don't show me."

She looked up with wide, stricken eyes. "Sixteen dead."

I held up a hand. "Any *good* news?"

"Parallel look-up protests have started. Central Park, Barcelona, Aspen. The PM of Sweden and the mayor of Newark have pledged support for us. The mayor of Newark is fasting."

"That's wonderful!"

She didn't look pleased.

"Put that down and come behold our people."

She joined me at the window, but without giving up the eddy, and at once was reabsorbed in the downtown footage.

"Chris," she said. "*Look.*"

I relented, but withstood only a glimpse. A middle-aged, dark-skinned man, shirt bloodied, unconscious, was swept to the curb by a water jet. Below, our peaceful cloud of supporters evolved in a slow, churning circle, singing, vociferating anyway, I couldn't hear. From Zoraida's eddy I heard *commentators*, whom I couldn't help imagining as part commentor, part tater-tot, analyzing: eddy was due to give its talk today. Meanwhile, the various protests seemed to have united—this sounded heartening—against the common enemy of the increasingly unrestrained riot police and their arriving military support.

Zoraida nudged the eddy into my line of sight.

Along the broad downtown avenue advanced what appeared to be a solid grey wall, stretching to the sidewalks where troopers drove protestors before their batons and shields. The wall moved forward, eyeless, featureless, through plumes of smoke. A scattering of black-clad people wearing hoods and gas masks dashed in and tossed something over it. They turned and ran back, faster than the wall, but were felled, en masse, in the road. The water washed them away.

"It's worse than last year," Zoraida said. She shut it off and held herself as though cold.

"Who were those people?"

"They looked like regular antifascists. At this point you can't say they're just LARPing anymore."

"We should leave," I said. "Fly up north. The aurora . . . For their sake," I explained to the look she gave me. Surely the comparative safety of our supporters down there was fleeting. And Zoraida herself should be spirited somewhere safe before it was really too late. "Don't you think they would go home, I mean, if we left?"

The activist shook her head, not in negation, but sorrowed recognition.

"Forget I said that," I said. "I'm learning."

CHAPTER THIRTY-ONE

H, I want you to know that I continue to respect the organization and its mission.

What was this? I preferred that blistering *To whom it may CONCERN* letter. She had apparently not sent it. I switched to camera. In the big glasses, in her little berth, she looked nauseous enough.

I'm sure you've been as horrified as I have with the protest footage, and I'm sure you're no more able than I am to sit on your hands. It must be hard at such a time to find yourself understaffed. If in fact you are contemplating a last-minute adjustment, I would like to offer whatever help I can from here, during this transition. I know your opinion of my abilities (separate I hope from your opinion of my character), and if there are any difficulties, please feel free to reach out to me one last time for input.

Yours sincerely,
Z

She erased the sincerely and sent it. I didn't like this. Her anxiety had plainly worsened—what these zealots, without her influence, her scruples, her logistical ingenuity, might attempt at short notice to rattle the delegates, empower the people. Despite our protective crowds below, she foreboded a miscarriage. On her screen, the downtown brutality resumed.

I faced the sky and wished that below was not a field but a lake, or rather a giant swimming pool, shallow enough that nobody could possibly drown.

Below the crystal rapids, we sipped our smoothies and watched the news. Eddy had given its talk. Barring surprises, the Egarp smart constitution would be ratified by the companies next day, locking the global economy into a new, eco-friendly, implacable order. Good for Palmer. It wouldn't do the trick, I supposed, but it was a graceful enough step toward a sincere, tardy togetherness. Curfew meanwhile was begun. Military vehicles patrolled lamplit, sign-strewn streets. Bereft of violence, the station resigned itself to its *look-up* reporter. The view, however, apparently from a camera raised on a van crane in our local road's shoulder, was unfortunate. The multitudes of the peaceful lay in darkness, while, in the foreground, illuminated by our own landing lights, ranks of armed officers stood braced. They must have been standing that way, tensed and laden, for hours now.

I had an idea. "Do you think we could declare a multilateral nap time down there? I think everyone would appreciate that."

Stoutmeier and his young disciples regarded me with awe. For a moment I missed Wade. Coverage shot back to downtown. Soldiers sprinted after a dark flicker in the costume of the no-longer-LARPing antifascists, but the scene they left behind remained briefly in the camera's eye, a barely intelligible, disorienting vision. As before, a water cannon sprayed bodies in the road. It stopped, and for a second one saw, everyone saw, that the people, or the sprawled remains of them among vests and helmets, were troopers. Clothes and skin were charred where not burned off, a hardly human heap.

I swallowed continuously until I'd mastered the acidic influx. Somehow the world of that time, the past century and a half of heaped corpses, hadn't prepared me for these half dozen. I seemed to waver from the room, as in the momentary shattering vertigo of not seeing yourself reflected in a mirror, before realizing it's not a mirror behind the bar but the other half of the restaurant. I got myself up to the observation deck and breathed.

Dotted with lantern light, with soft eddy light, with colored fairy lights, our pasture lay in peace. Ahead, like buzzards, helicopters circled the city, search beams conic in haze. I watched as one drew closer and closer, until it swept over our field a bright disc of people covering their eyes. Even from within the stout dome the sound was intense, far louder than our own helicopters, as though one of these things were directly in front of me, and a moment later I was lost in light. After it strayed off, I guided myself by the rail, not waiting to fully regain sight, back toward the stairs.

But around the starboard curve, I found the others, aglow and dead still, backs to the beam. It must have been mere yards away, deafening, motionless. Jake alone had bent over and pulled down his pants. After a minute, the light moved on, sweeping the deck around to stern. The rhythmic roar of the blades, not unlike a fusillade, shrank and expanded as it orbited back.

"Come on," Stoutmeier said, rushing his round bulk to the stair door and holding it open while the rest of us ran through.

We stood on the steps, panting, waiting for the sound to go, staring around at one another. If there was an agreeable, adrenalized edge to the fright, I couldn't detect it. The din faded, and Stoutmeier cracked the door open. After another minute, we emerged, walking together around the full circumference. Our two great fields were just as they were. The lamentable road was as before. It was getting late.

"Sit for a second," said Zoraida, cocooned in my covers.

I sat, resting a hand on her shoulder. We were quiet.

"What are you thinking about?" I asked.

"Honestly?" she said. "Right this second, a cheeseburger."

"And what kind of cheese will you have on that?"

"Cheddar," she said. "With fries. Also cheddar on the fries. And, if I'm baring my soul here, mayonnaise."

"Anything to drink?"

"Not a smoothie. That's all I ask. What were you thinking about?"

"Oh goodness knows. Besides wondering what you were thinking about, probably the aurora borealis."

She didn't respond, and I just sat there, gradually lightening the pressure of my hand.

A bang awoke me. It was still dark. I dumped myself out of the hammock and started inside. Zoraida's silhouette was already making for the window. Our lights were on, but we couldn't see the ground. The air was dense with shrapnel or some particulate. Falling away, it caught the light, and for a moment I thought it was simply beautiful.

Then I realized it was simply beautiful. In the landing

lights scintillated a veil of tiny, still points before the whole blew like a scarf or nation of dyed starlings, and then again seemed to hang motionless and winking before sifting down. Confetti. Another bang, the escape hatch over my quarters, from which Jake had unloaded his secret cloud. Through the descending glitter we could now make out the visors looking up, as the red, blue, purple, green, covered them.

CHAPTER THIRTY-TWO

I MUST HAVE MANAGED to sleep again, because here was Zoraida above my hammock, talking into her eddy, squinting. It was day.

"I *don't know*," she was saying. "He's right here." She handed me the eddy.

"Hello?"

"Curtis? What's the matter with you? Why aren't you answering your goddamn eddy?" It took me a moment to realize it was Morgan Palmer. I had never heard him speak with such natural annoyance.

"My sleep," I explained, "was rather picturesquely interrupted . . ."

My pupils adjusted to the light. Over downtown Charlotte stood a wide column of smoke, like a volcano had erupted.

"Morgan!" I cried. "Are you all right over there? What happened?"

"Some *motherfucking* radicals blew up half a block. My bed flipped over. We're in a basement. We're fine, but these agents are not taking it lightly, and they've been expressing an interest in your circus over there. You have to stop it now. Get out. Get everyone out. Are you registering? Just go. I'm hanging up."

"Wait. Out to where? What's happening?"

"I don't know what's happening. I've just been interrogated about that supposed security threat we didn't respond to. They're pretending to think it's the same people and that you all may be in cahoots. They've had casualties, and they have to make a move. You can guess how popular your little protest is here now that it's not so little. They're not going to let it get bigger, not after this. Have you really not been boarded yet? I've been calling for an hour."

"Boarded?"

"Just get everyone *safely* out of there. Please."

"Yes, yes. Thank you, Palmer. Good luck."

"Handle this, Curtis. Please. I want to see you in Florham Park."

He was a good fellow, Palmer. It had to be admitted. I returned the eddy to Zoraida, staring at the smoke.

"Oh god," she whispered. "I knew it. Those idiots. Those inflexible *idiots*. Is he all right?"

"Goldfarb, get us out of here. Away from the city. North."

Or had Palmer meant for us to use parachutes? We lurched away, accompanied by a great din of rotors.

"Is that us?" I asked. I hadn't heard that sound before.

"I don't know."

"He's all right," I said.

I rose from the hammock and looked down.

It had begun. The official story, we would hear, was that the protestors started it. Now they fled in a swirling tide, those nearer the road falling like skittles as troops rolled over the field.

We didn't turn away or speak until the pasture was a brown ragged cloud to the south between a patch of woods and the highway. I had been aware the while of a commotion, the vibration of feet coming and going, and I imagined the others, woken or otherwise startled by our sudden departure, seeing the plume over the city and the incipient massacre below, running around in alarm. I was preparing to go make some explanation, when, evidently not expecting to find anyone behind the door on which they didn't care to knock, a spurt of armored beings came rushing in, after the briefest startled hesitation, owing as much to the condition of the room as its occupants, pistols drawn, shouting as if on the verge of terror themselves.

I had thought there were at least half a dozen, but it seemed there were only three. They must have come to us from more fraught conditions, the present stampede amounting to a sort of inapt continuation. Their urgency, as if my bedroom might be harboring armed renegades, was so out of proportion to the circumstance I had trouble responding in any way, even with panic. One fellow seized me as if I were someone of fearsome strength, and another flung himself on Zoraida as if she were a live grenade, contriving in the struggle to tear her sleep shirt, an ancient item of mine, the revealed flash, under that mass of man and protective gear, tender and threatened as the exposed interior of an animal slit down the torso.

The third officer, after satisfying himself there were no hidden dangers in the bathroom and closets, came to a stop in front of us. This young man's eyes, puffy and over-bright, an oil fire of wakefulness floating on deep fatigue, roved Zoraida, now upright, hands pinned behind her back, and then me with plain admiration.

"*Fuck you*," he observed appreciatively. He was really very young. Born to other circumstances he could have been a Sky

Yacht intern. He looked around the room, amazed at the filth, and back and forth between lovely Zoraida and unlovely me. "Who the fuck are you?"

I didn't answer.

"You must be *someone*, hitting that," meaning Zoraida, "and *here* . . ." meaning my appalling mess. He was not on the path, and his black boot depressed a paperback aslant on some other object so it bent painfully.

All I managed to say was, "We don't talk like that here." It sounded insane. The kid of course laughed.

"Who the fuck are *you*?" Zoraida erupted.

She had not stopped struggling. Her face was deep red, neck blotched. Saliva flew. "That's Chris fucking Curtis! Now show some ID and a warrant before you lose your sorry ass fascist fake army jobs faster than he can pick up an eddy. In fact, why don't you joyriding dickless sheep take your fucking antidote or whatever it is and have a nap before the only people you'll be able to molest are your fellow inmates. It's a nice mattress, I can tell you."

This last insinuation was meant only to rub the fellow's comparative inconsequence in his face. He absorbed it with good cheer. "We may see about that," he said. Then abruptly, to the man holding me, "Take him out."

"Tell them, Chris! Tell them what you are. We're not leaving. This isn't a fucking war zone. It's his yacht. It's private property. Warrant. ID. Tell them."

"Gentlemen . . ."

But reality was in the room. Clearly, simply. It had pierced my Sky Yacht like a child's dirty finger popping a soap bubble.

"Gentlemen," I said, "please, we'll go peacefully."

"What?" Zoraida's said, eyes wide. "I thought you were

going to *starve*. Remember that? Is this the world suddenly becoming *hospitable*? Do something! Call your lawyers, if that's what you do. Stand up!" To the kid, "Get your boss on the line. Trust me. You're in over your heads here."

It's possible every fiber in her being was not telling her, deafeningly, that we were in real danger. Or the roar was gratefully drowning another voice which had been saying, all this time, you're not doing enough, you're not enough. Or maybe this was just what real courage looked like. Like madness. With effort I managed to enunciate, "We're all over-excited. We don't want undue trouble."

The soldier nodded, and I was carried from the room.

Only when the door clicked behind, dividing me and my escort from Zoraida and the other two, did I begin to flail. As I yelled I don't know what, the officer or whatever he was cuffed my wrists and began pulling me along in the direction of the education wing. Another person appeared, hailing us from behind. He wore no helmet or other gear over his dark blue uniform. He walked swiftly, swinging a limp cap. He was grey at the sides, tan on top, neck lizardy. The younger one went rigid in salute.

"I'll take Mr. Curtis from here."

The kid snapped down his hand and left us.

"Cuffs," the older man called him back.

"Wait," I panted. "Zoraida."

With a sympathetic murmur of negation, he went on leading me away, uncuffed, gently, by the upper arm, as if we were two old emigres out strolling a windy Fifth Avenue.

"Stop," I said.

"You're not hurt?" the man asked with concern, not stopping.

I would have cried if I spoke. I wasn't hurt. Asking permission with my eyes, I took out my eddy. He assented.

I expected only to hear, the camera facing the floor or ceiling.

I was not wholly unaware that unspeakable abuses, especially toward women, were frequent and even routine where ordinary human considerations could be relaxed for higher purposes—war, riots, traffic incidents—when, as if in a dream, without any stab of conscience, the man can do to another whatever he desires. Our greatest atrocities probably had their origin, whatever the purported ideals, only in the appeal of this hideous relaxation. I was aware that whole villages of innocents were brutalized in the most inhuman ways, daily, even up to the moment. I had seen in the U.S. the constantly replenished footage of police brutality, and last night's charred police bodies, and yet it seemed I didn't quite believe any of it, all the while without realizing I didn't quite believe it, as you know very well but don't truly believe that in not so long you'll be an elderly, helpless invalid soon to die. Not until looking at my eddy then did I understand that such things could happen in any relation to me, innocuous, floating Chris Curtis.

Zoraida's upper half filled the screen, prone on my blanket, her head twisted sideways with one of my own cashmere socks, balled up, distending her mouth, elbows out behind her, protruding from the torn old sleep shirt like bony wings, wrists not cuffed but for some reason zip-tied together at the lower back. The voice of the kid who had ordered me removed was saying, "Just unlock it and prove us wrong." He referred to her eddy, which he was evidently holding. The reverse camera showed him, his boyish, red-eyed face. It was true that unless she unlocked her eddy it would remain inaccessible to any authority, and perhaps this sort of coercion had become more common than was widely known in cases where no other witness was present. But the eddy stuff was mostly pretext. The boy repeated his insincere exhortation. I switched cameras, and Zoraida's poor, gagged face zoomed up as the eddy was presented to her.

"What is this?" The question came from the man leading me. "That's her eddy. Did that chimpanzee of a contract officer butt dial you?" He looked for one moment confused, angry, and then it dawned on him. "You have access. My god. Where are they?"

We ran together to my door.

CHAPTER THIRTY-THREE

THE BOYS ON EITHER side of Zoraida clattered upright and saluted.

"You're both done," said my friend flatly. With some difficulty he got the sock out of Zoraida's mouth. She suffered a fit of coughing as he cut the zip ties. "Find your things," the man said gently, and to the others, "Turn away." He himself walked down the path to the window, did not look out. His gaze instead seemed to inventory the mess of notebooks and such on the floor.

Watching the diminished cloud over the now far-off city, I waited in some suspense for Zoraida to regain breath enough to shout whatever almighty vituperations she would. She'd have inferred more agency than I could take credit for in my swift return with a superior, and, her threats vindicated, I imagined she would let those two wretches have it as few have had it, and, I hoped, in a moment of inspiration, kick both groins with all her might.

I'm ashamed to say I was surprised at the silence that followed, and when I turned back to find her dressed in her own clothes, hovering over the bed, not looking at the officers or myself but dimly straight ahead as though no longer tenanted by her own soul, a surge of outrage and then compensatory purpose filled me, puffed me with desperate consequence, until all through myself I was shouting, I am a rich, important man, and as I live I will not permit anything to touch this poor girl again, and she'll have everything she ever wants and ever wanted. I, Chris Curtis, will see to it. And after another moment I was able to think, hearteningly, that when they did manage to bring their case against Zoraida, this appalling, thankfully abortive episode could work in her favor, could possibly make the difference.

The older officer may have been thinking on these lines too, for he asked, "Do you want to go to a hospital?"

She shook her head.

"Just say if you change your mind. Now we do have to be moving. After you, Miss Simpson."

She shook her head again. My heart bobbed and sank. She was back, to a degree, she was in there. That was the bob.

"I'm sorry to insist," said the officer, "but we believe you all are in danger here. Once the bomb sniffers have gone over the craft, you'll be welcome to return to it, assuming all else is in order."

Her voice came out hoarsely, weakly, weighted with a new, weary authority. "You could at least have the grace to not insult our intelligence. Arrest us, shoot us," she flapped a hand, "whatever you're going to do. Or, goodbye."

"Zoraida!" I cried. "We'll have a chance to address this, but now these fellows here . . . Just now, this isn't . . ."

It must have been obvious that our compliance would not be a factor in whether we were still on the Sky Yacht in five minutes. We wouldn't be. The government and its unopposable armed force, a considerable defunding of which we ourselves had called for in our demands, wanted us gone from the Sky Yacht, probably from existence, and this moment of comparative civility was fragile. Our protest against every entrenched domestic power had shown signs of catching on, and these powers could no longer rely on some radical group to blow us out of the sky for them. The blast downtown, whether or not they had intelligence connecting someone aboard to the blasters, was pretext enough. Of course they would have to quell and discredit us. A pair of scrawny unarmed beings would not be an obstacle. We were at their mercy and could transmute again, at any moment, from human beings to resistors. Once in custody, down in some dreary, official place, my station might be of some avail—in those times, wealth remained, thankfully, the chief determinant in legal outcomes—but now, in the disorder of my room, it was just silly to resist. Looking at Zoraida, I saw she understood this, and I saw that not resisting wasn't what she was here for. She stood maniacally, magnificently firm.

"You have our full cooperation," I said. "Zoraida may not be in a state to comply due to the immediate traumatic aftermath of that vicious attack. We'll leave, but under your personal supervision," I added to the superior officer.

He took Zoraida by the arm, and seeing she was alone, without recourse, and at last completely exhausted, she moved. I won't say it didn't hurt to see her leave that way. Passing me, she mustered, "Thank you, Chris," with some part, I've always thought afterward, sincerity, and slid me a long, sincere glance, like a returned ring across a table.

The elevator we rode to the loading bay was all mirrors and everywhere you caught yourself regressing into corners of space.

The older man directed me to a small, clear helicopter crouched beside a big, olive-colored one into the belly of which the dozen brave interns were being loaded. Already seated on its bare floor were the round shapes of Stoutmeier and Jake, and another, which from the straight back and adroitly folded legs I took for the headmistress. We paused to watch Zoraida loaded and safely buckled in beside her. A hand directed my head into the smaller chopper.

My man buckled me into an embracing leather seat and eased back into one opposite. He indicated a headset hanging beside me, big olive ear cups and a microphone. I put it on and saw he was speaking, but I heard nothing. Maybe he was talking to someone else. We rose, and a moment later the bigger, twin-rotor helicopter rose over the dome of the Sky Yacht. Remaining on the pad was one last military helicopter. Banking north, I had a glimpse of my topmost pool, the two empty floats bumping the sides.

CHAPTER THIRTY-FOUR

I WATCHED THE OTHERS being unloaded into the dazed earthly noon between bland administrative buildings. I was in a sort of conference space: long grey table with one empty, capsized to-go cup, frugal mesh swivel chairs, white walls relieved by a single framed poster, a sprawling, sepia-toned elm tree. I was, it seemed, all right. I don't say that if I'd had a cyanide pill in a locket I wouldn't have swallowed it, but my long training in ignoring the world and my life left me equipped to dwell little on the circumstance, in fact *unable* to dwell on it, or to have any but the most trivial, inopportune thoughts. It would all get me, wallop me, but at a delay. In the immediate crisis, it remained sealed up, swelling but contained, floating just outside my perception, like the Sky Yacht floating on without me, lost, subjected to the rifling and trifling of soldiers and sniffing, sightless machines.

I had been deposited here and for the moment abandoned. My eddy gazed glassily back, and once more I seemed to be saying, *help, eddy. Give me something I know you can't*. I checked Camera View. Unsurprisingly an error alert appeared. I was no longer in range of the Sky Yacht network. I wanted to see Zoraida, to set myself right with her, to hear her voice back in full, high force, berating me.

I might yet read her words, her journal, one of her splendid, spirited tirades, or, better, create an emu from that wealth of data, but the documents too were lost behind an error alert. My officer returned. Did I need anything? "Where is Zoraida being taken?" I demanded.

"You tell me," this suave reptile said, easing into a swivel chair opposite. "I always figured eddy had some backdoor access, but I did not guess the extent of it." He raised his brows and coughed, impressed with the extent of it. "Don't worry. Your secret is safe, for now. We will have to see what you have though."

With this I would not comply. By that time it was as good as inscribed on Moses's tablets that the Fifth Amendment protected a person from being compelled to unlock his eddy. This man could legally seize it and throw everything in his power at unlocking it from now to the end of time, which was apparently how long it would take by all known strategies, but he couldn't make me do it.

"You can't compel me to unlock my eddy. Everyone knows that."

He nodded, as if pained at this failure of fellowship. A rueful gravity bagged under his eyes.

"That protection," he said, "applies to personal, potentially incriminating data. Surveillance footage, or data you gather on your *customers*, is another story. As a third party, you can't withhold that from a criminal investigation. Ask your legal team when they get here. We know you were surveilling Zoraida Simpson, and I presume it wasn't just her. I have a warrant in process."

"I might as well tell you it's no use. It only worked with the Sky Yacht network. I just checked."

"We saw you just check."

I resisted the reflex to look for the camera.

"We're bringing the Sky Yacht here now," he said. "Or trying. You wouldn't have a resource on that for us?"

"I don't seem to have the manual with me."

"We'd appreciate a technical contact. My guys up there are experienced aviators, but the Sky Yacht is . . ." he grinned for some reason, "to put it mildly, a unique craft."

"Oh I think the flight path is all programmed long in advance. My late partner was, to put it mildly, a control freak. The security measures are fairly thorough. He handled it all himself. He was really quite—"

"But there must be some contingency measure, in case, for example . . ."

"Oh maybe Palmer had clearance," I said. "Probably."

"We tried Mr. Palmer."

"Not cooperative?" I could imagine.

The man shook his head. "Better you than me having to deal with that cocky shit. Of course, he wasn't aware of the present situation. He wasn't in the know about your own *thorough security measures*, was he? I didn't think so. A little secret between the founders. Now, Mr. Curtis, I find it hard to credit that you yourself had no access to the craft's systems."

"Oh, yes, I have—had—access, if you want to call it that, but I can't help you with the technicalities. I would just tell Goldfarb if I wanted something. Goldfarb is really the one in charge."

"This is the system computer?"

"I liked to think of him as the pilot, with a neat white hat, a mustache . . ."

"Is this Goldfarb imprinted on just your biometrics?"

"And Wade's of course."

"I assume you have to be in-network for this too? Well," the man sighed, sweeping his cap off the table, "two birds. Sorry to bring you all the way here and turn around, but I didn't have full command of the facts. Your legal team is welcome to join us, of course. Up for another ride when they get here?"

"Never mind my legal team!" I tried to look merely decisive, whereas, by some heavenly oversight, my ferry across the Styx, halfway out, had about-faced, and rising before me was the living shore. Even if only for the hour. Time anyway to think. Perhaps, if my affable psychopomp was well pleased, a float in my old pool . . .

Already my old pool.

"I'm all yours," I said, standing.

The return took twice as long as the evacuation, owing to the Yacht's continued northward progress. All the while, seated opposite, my officer, who had probably told me his name, talking busily to someone I couldn't hear and plugging away at his eddy and another contraption, did not look out at a low line of behemoths, bottoms flat, tops towering up in endless, boiling ramifications, sun-glazed and solid. The autopilot brought us gently to rest beside the big troop transporter we had left here earlier. Disembarking, I resisted kissing the very ground of the helipad, and we passed through the airlock into the great, silent warmth.

After a *bio-break*, we would reconvene in my office. This restroom here, he could enjoy, and I my own, as I wanted to gather some things anyway, an old notebook of poetry . . . I expected some resistance, but after all there was no chance of my running far, I had already demonstrated unlooked-for cooperation, and my friend allowed me the dignity of going to my own bathroom unescorted.

My rooms were not in chaos so much as ruin, ransacked. It took some time to find a swimsuit.

The observation deck was abandoned as ever, and none saw me ascend the spiral stair to my topmost pool. The Yacht had gained little altitude since our rushed departure—I had neglected to tell Goldfarb to go up in addition to north—and what clouds there were floated high above.

"Goldfarb!" I cried. "I'm back. Now kindly raise us to those clouds up there."

While we rose, once more I checked Zoraida's eddy. Camera View remained unavailable, the target eddy being outside the Sky Yacht network, but the documents, no doubt stored on the network's *cloud*, as the unfortunate usage of the time had it, were again viewable. Her diary had no additions since last seen, or any additions hadn't made their way here. Possibly her eddy hadn't been returned to her. I dashed a message to Palmer, just to be sure the great eddy legal apparatus had been deployed with all gusto on her behalf, and on that of the others, along with whatever help my own resources could supply. Even so, I wasn't easy about Zoraida. I returned in mind to that silent elevator, trying to catch a last glance among the reflected madhouse slivers. Our deal had been that she would leave intact, and I don't think it anticipated my being removed by force. How incriminating really were these documents I was to hand over? I imagined the worst of it was that Humans application essay.

On review it was, undeniably, suggestive. That business especially about a return to Gilded Age inequality calling for a return of the Emma Goldmans and Lucy Parsons and their

Gilded Age anarchist weapon of choice. And then there were her unhappy views on individual action and self-sacrifice, though these might suggest an exculpatory emotional imbalance. I read again:

> The greatest threat is the threat to our indefiniteness. The greatest tragedy is to lose it partway . . . What does one half of a big, flabby, tepid, protected life go for? . . . Are we really having such a good time here? If we were, would we deserve it?

I tried not to see the empty float beside mine, where in gratitude for my sacrifice and perhaps in kinship, she had lain with me in the sky. I would have thrown it right out of the water but for fear its flight to the observation deck would call attention to my hideout. Suddenly it was darker, then brighter.

We had ascended through the continent of cloud, and, turning prone, I looked down once more on the sun-capped spires of that immaculate, unsuspected world, and tried to feel as I had before, relieved, if not of solitude, of gravity. I flipped over, onto my back. We were in fact in one of my beloved cloud archipelagos, rising toward higher, looming shrines. My float spun gently beneath, and now that infernal antenna came jarringly into view.

"Goddamn it!" I blurted.

Almost at once, up the stairs clattered heavy boots. Crowding the small metal landing were three officers, followed shortly by my friend, wearing a look of bemused, parental disappointment. One of the three younger ones had been in the room with Zoraida, the quieter one. He was apparently not yet *done*.

"Mr. Curtis," said the captain, with something of the old Palmer-esque forbearance. "I understand it's been a stressful day, but I would appreciate that you keep us informed of your whereabouts. Now, would you like to take us to the servers and transfer the data to one of our secure machines, or if you prefer we could take your eddy and bring it back when we're done, leaving you in peace."

It struck me that with my spying app I might somehow delete the records.

"May I have a few more moments to recover my equilibrium?" I ventured. "Half an hour?"

"I have to insist. We'll just take the eddy and bring it right back."

I paddled over with one hand. If only we hadn't made eddies waterproof. Well, even if I refused to unlock it, no doubt the so-called cloud was only a computer somewhere aboard from which these fellows could get what they needed, although, pitting this lot against Wade's paranoid savant security measures, I imagined not very quickly, possibly not within weeks—possibly not at all. One learned not to underestimate Wade. I stopped paddling and seemed, once more, to dither.

"Mr. Curtis, we'd like to get back to headquarters by end of day."

The efficient, uniformed, Kevlar-vested men stared at the dodderer in the pool, the slight, bare torso, the eminently wringable neck.

"Would you say, gentlemen," I wondered aloud, "that we're having a good enough time here?"

The older man pushed out an uncertain chuckle. "Mr. Curtis, I appreciate your fondness for this place, but—"

"I mean, are we really having such a good time?" I persisted.

"Mr. Curtis—"

"No, I suppose you're right. I wouldn't say so. I encourage you fellows to relax a bit on the observation deck. We still have quite a lot of nutritious smoothie ingredients."

"We will be asking for your cooperation now," the man said, firmly. "It's possible I wasn't clear that this is your legal obligation. Failure to cooperate is a crime."

"A crime . . ."

"That I assure you will be prosecuted regardless of your position."

"I believe you," I said. "But while we're here, I mean, before that, you might as well enjoy yourself. Goldfarb, I think seal the airlock, at least until we reach the North. The aurora . . ." At the Sky Yacht's leisurely airspeed, I estimated it would be at least a month or two before we ran out of gas. "And just to be safe," I considered, "have a look at those choppers on the pad and raise us to an altitude where they can't take off. They're just a troop transporter and a luxury type thing, nothing I would think built for especially high flying."

I dropped my gaze from the clouds for a brief, delicious glance at the faces on the landing. "Now then," I said, "off we go."

I was pleased not to find myself immediately manhandled. For the moment, the captain merely began, "You understand what this will mean for you—"

"Oh for me," I said. "Please don't bother yourself about me. Try to relax. As we ascend, for instance, I'd like to call your attention to this particular cloud structure, my favorite at middle altitudes, the archipelago . . ."

There would be, as I knew there would be, some terrible difficulty about all this in the end, but they didn't get their evidence, and with the fearsome eddy legal apparatus behind her, Zoraida was back to the needful world within months.

I would be longer, much longer, but now a perfect silence seemed to swell as we rose to another blue, interrupted only by that old infernal antenna, behind which a scrap of cloud, whose birth I had just missed, gathered its glowing vapors and sailed.

Acknowledgements

Thank you, Trout Family: Lauren Belski, Wythe Marschall, CJ Hauser, Erin Harte, Steve Aubrey, James Donovan, Helen Rubinstein, Wes Mattingly, Michael Donkin. Thank you, Jenny Offill. Thanks, Stephanie Greenwood, and Ilya Lyashevsky. Thanks to Byrdcliffe Art Colony, where much of this was written, and the residencies at MASS MoCA and ChaNorth. Thank you, the artist Skye Gilkerson, and Wilder, for making life more or less hospitable.

David Greenwood's stories have appeared in *Electric Literature*, *Fence*, *Tin House* online and elsewhere. He has a degree in computer science from Boston University, and an MFA from Brooklyn College, where he won the Himan Brown award for fiction. His ongoing micro-novels project, *The Bubble Cannon*, can be found at davidgreenwood.substack.com.